FOOD FOR THOUGHT

SARA MADDERSON

For Chris, Paddy & Tilly.

You are my whole world.

1

The gods have at their disposal two tools that titillate them and torment us. The first is the curveball. We wake up each morning with no inkling as to what may lie ahead that day. We may as well be running blindfolded through life, never knowing when we'll run smack into a brick wall.

The second is the real masterstroke. The gods blinker us, ensuring our complete inability to judge whether the curveballs they throw at us are as they seem. Apparent catastrophes may, only years later, be understood as the blessings they really are, and vice versa. We have this clarity only when the gods finally take pity on us and throw us a bone, and the bone is hindsight.

Evelyn Macleod's curveball would come on a seemingly inauspicious day. It was the Friday heading into the late May bank holiday weekend, and the uncharacteristically good weather forecast boded as well for the economy as it did for the spirits of the Great British public. Across the country, workers would spend the day mentally checking out, messaging their mates to exchange boozy plans, and staring impatiently out of the window rather than at their screens.

For Evelyn, however, it was business as usual. By 7.30am she had already completed a thirty minute online bootcamp workout and a twenty-minute meditation practice, recited her daily affirmations, journalled on both her goals and her reasons for gratitude, read a chapter of a book on productivity, checked and answered emails, showered, blow-dried her long, sleek, chestnut hair, dressed, applied a face-full of makeup whose natural, dewy effect belied her skills, taken her probiotics and allowed herself her daily cup of Bulletproof coffee blended with grass-fed butter.

Breakfast wouldn't feature in Evelyn's morning. She adhered to a strict intermittent fasting regime on weekdays, eating only in an eight-hour window between 12 noon and 8pm. She would break her fast (coffee excluded) with lunch.

Evelyn loved mornings, loved what they represented. She couldn't comprehend people who hit snooze when the alarm went off and burrowed grumblingly under the covers to resist the dawn of a new day. Mornings were precious, pure, unsullied. Each morning represented a fresh start, a virgin day, a slate magically wiped clean of the previous day's failures and disappointments. Everything seemed better in the morning. Evelyn believed fervently that if you won your morning, you won your day. She knew, and despaired, that somewhere deep within her lurked a monster of utter slothfulness. She never allowed it out, and instead took great pains to keep her eye on the prize and ignore that concealed, parallel version of herself who would jump at the chance to spend a day on the sofa, binge-watching Netflix, eating chocolate biscuits and sabotaging everything that she had worked so hard for. Instead, she focused on approaching each day as the gigantic opportunity that it was.

Her husband, Seb, had left the house early. Evelyn was married to Seb Macleod, the charismatic celebrity chef and CEO of his vast eponymous food empire. Most households in the UK boasted one or two of his cookbooks, and people would get to know the power-couple even better that month, when they picked up their copy of *Food* magazine and saw them on the cover, smiling in what their PR team intended to be an aspirational but accessible fashion. The tagline read *The Beckhams of the Food World.*

Seb was certainly the face of their operation—a talented, charming TV chef with a gorgeous smile, a high-energy persona and an obsession with celebrating the best, freshest produce. However, as both his Chief Content Officer and Chief Marketing Officer, Evelyn was tasked with building his brand and steering it in a new direction.

As the world had got more health conscious and consumers went crazy for keto, paleo and veganism, Evelyn had noticed that some celebrity chefs were getting left behind by sticking to what they knew best—pasta, sandwiches, roasts, and cakes. They were being quickly overtaken by a new wave of wellness bloggers and vloggers. She'd lobbied hard to persuade the team that they should pivot to focus more on health-conscious recipes, while continuing to keep the freshest, tastiest ingredients front-and-centre of their brand.

Her bet paid off. As terms like 'organic', 'biodynamic', 'pasture-raised' and 'high-welfare' became industry buzzwords, Seb Macleod Limited increased its sourcing team, invested in an in-house functional practitioner and nutritionist, and broadened their scope to partner with worthy allies, from soil associations to oncologists. They had closed a Series C round of funding the previous year and opened their first Malibu-inspired café, Seb's Kitchen, to serve up turmeric lattes to the well-heeled of Westbourne Grove. Keeping the juggernaut moving forward was an enormous amount of work, but Seb and Evelyn were well-matched in their work ethic. Thanks to their laser-focus, the company was flourishing.

The mirrors in Evelyn's palatial Holland Park dressing-room afforded her a three-sixty view of herself. She gave the multiple reflections a quick once-over and nodded. Good. She would do. Her tightly tailored, khaki boiler suit was chic enough for the office and comfortable enough to drive to Kent in later. Geometrical gold jewellery elevated the look, and she could bomb around London in her flat leather Loewe sandals. Grabbing the shoes, she padded barefoot downstairs.

In the kitchen, her eight-year-old son, Eddie, was sitting at the vast marble island. He tucked into scrambled eggs and avocado on toast while one of their housekeepers, Maria, hovered attentively by the double sink.

"Good morning, Maria. Good morning, Eddilicious!" Evelyn exclaimed. God, he really was delicious. Just look at him. He was a sight for sore eyes, gorgeously golden and typically dishevelled despite Maria's best efforts with the hairbrush. She scooted around the island, dropped the sandals and took his face in her hands, kissing his sticky mouth and inhaling his beautiful, little-boy smell.

'How are you, Angel-face? Did you sleep well? One more day at school and then you're on half-term for a week, lucky boy!'

'Hi Mummy!' Eddie sang. He'd inherited his father's blue eyes and obscene eyelashes, but his hair, which was darkening steadily as he grew, was still caramel-coloured.

Nevertheless, he was a chip off the old block. He gave her a huge, devastating beam that lit up the room.

His words tumbled out. 'Mummy, are you picking me up early to go to Kent? Don't forget to bring my iPad and my snacks for the car. And please can I have my Minecraft water bottle? I don't like my Batman one any more. When we get to Auntie Jess' house can I sleep in Mike's bunk-bed with him? Will you tell Mr Solomon that I need to leave early today so we can go on holiday?'

'I will not!' laughed Evelyn. 'I'll pick you up at normal time; we'll still make it down to Kent for dinner. I'm sure Maria will kindly pack up the right water bottle for you. And we mustn't forget to pack Bunny.' She caught Maria's eye and smiled. 'Right little guy, eat up this yummy breakfast and then you and I can put Bunny in your rucksack before we head to school.'

ONCE SHE'D DROPPED Eddie at school, she doubled back and headed to her office in White City. Eddie had skipped practically the whole way through Holland Park to his prep school in Notting Hill. He'd held her hand, pulling the whole left side of her body down whenever he skipped. She'd been on the verge of asking him to cut it out when she realised how extraordinary it was that kids his age rarely walked—they skipped or scampered. How wonderful it must be to exist in such a constant state of elation that one had to express it by leaping about on the street.

Nevertheless, she had to admit that she shared Eddie's sense of supreme wellbeing that morning. It was hard not to, walking through the leafy avenues and crescents of west London, with their ice cream-coloured houses and perfectly manicured gardens. Their own house was a particularly fine specimen on an exclusive street, but it didn't stop her keen aesthetic sense from appreciating the surrounding beauty. All felt good in the world on mornings like this. Surely May was the most intoxicating month of all, with everything so intensely *green*, seemingly out of nowhere, and birdsong filling the air? It was extraordinary the extent to which you came back to life in spring, having not quite grasped how much you'd died inside over winter.

Evelyn loved walking around London, particularly in the warmer months. Seb teased her about it. You can use my driver, he'd told her, umpteen times. But the idea creeped her out. Lovely as Seb's driver, Roy, was, she hated the idea of him ferrying her around between school and work, while she felt obliged to make awkward conversation or pretend to be busy with something. And it wasn't even like she could work in the back of the car; she felt nauseous whenever she tried to read in any moving vehicle. It was far preferable to her to walk whenever possible, and then when she needed to use one of the cars she would drive herself, thank you very much.

Adding to her sense of wellbeing was the upcoming weekend in Kent. While her conscious mind ran through the work-day ahead, her subconscious luxuriated in the knowledge of the imminent escape. Evelyn, Seb and Eddie were due to spend the long weekend staying at Sorrel Farm, an idyllic working farm, resort and all-round foodie heaven in north Kent. Even better, Sorrel Farm was the brainchild of Evelyn's oldest and closest friend, Jess. Over the last few years, Jess had transformed her family's farm into a luxury resort with the help of her wife, Zoe.

Evelyn and Jess had met and become inseparable at school. After many years of appearing to enjoy the male species very much, Jess had spent some time in France post graduation and fallen for the love of her life and her soulmate, Zoe. Zoe was traffic-stoppingly beautiful and terrifyingly clever, a statuesque, bilingual genius who'd studied Theology at Oxford before returning to her native Provence and training to be a chef.

Funnily enough, Seb had never fully hit it off with Jess and Zoe. Evelyn suspected a combination of intellectual arrogance—Seb could be pretty snooty about the levels of professional success he'd achieved compared to less famous chefs—and a vague, low-level homophobia, or at least social awkwardness around gay people. No surprise there; Seb had boarded at one of Britain's top single-sex public schools, and an inability to maturely manage emotional or sexual issues was practically guaranteed at those places.

Nevertheless, Seb had fallen in line with her plans for a leisurely few days in the bucolic Kentish countryside, and she was grateful for his support. Lord knew, they would benefit from some low-key family time away from the circus.

When Evelyn turned up at the Seb Macleod Limited HQ, she saw through the enormous glass doors that Seb was wrapping up a breakfast workshop for the press in their dedicated events area. It was a huge, double-height space boasting floor-to-ceiling windows, white floors and walls, a large white island around which a select assortment of journalists and bloggers sat on bar stools, and an enormous, vibrant green living wall. The effect of the vast white space and the pops of colour from the wall and the bountiful fresh food on the island was striking. The greenery framed Seb as he entertained the guests. Evelyn could tell by his body language, and that of the journalists, that he had them eating out of the palm of his hand.

He looked gorgeous, as usual—tall, tanned, lithe, his dark hair swept back with a few loose strands falling over his eyes. He'd rolled up the sleeves of his pale blue linen shirt, and a chef's apron covered him from the waist down. Evelyn watched him flash his famous smile at some of the females around him and, if how they were leaning in towards him was any indication, it seemed to be working. He was flirting. That was fine; that charisma was a key part of his brand, and of what had made him such a success. She watched him fix one woman with those flashing blue eyes as he grinned at her and handed her a spoon of something to try, and the woman squirmed delightedly on her stool. He had that Clinton-esque ability to make you feel like the only person in the room when he focused his attention on you, and boy was it an effective skill.

Evelyn loved watching Seb in action. She felt like a voyeur. She knew that right now, the room was in thrall to him and that everyone would leave that breakfast invigorated for their day ahead. It wasn't just the delicious wholefoods that he'd served up, or the signed copy of his latest book, *Honest Food*, tucked into their goodie bags, but also the particular energy that he radiated. His passion, his flair, and some indefinable aura all drew people to him and fed those people's needs. She spotted it wherever they went; she guessed they called it star quality.

And yet, at the end of the day, he was hers. When the press and the adoring fans had gone, it was she who would go home with him, strolling hand-in-hand back to Holland Park if they both got out of the office at the same time. It often hit her like an entirely fresh revelation, as if she couldn't quite believe it, as though it were too potent to keep a constant grasp of. Often in her dreams, she was single, alone. She would awake and hear his breathing, and the relief at coming face to face with her reality would break over her like a wave.

Reluctantly she turned away from the charming tableau beyond the doors and headed for her office. Time to stop perving over her husband and do some work.

AN HOUR LATER, she looked up as Seb burst through her office door. Gone was the relaxed manner and the easy smile. His face was drained of colour, and his eyes were frantic.

'Ev, darling,' he said, 'I have to talk to you about something. Now.'

2

Seb slammed the door shut behind him. He hit a switch, and the glass walls of Evelyn's goldfish-bowl office immediately turned opaque. She watched in alarm as he strode over to the sofa and sank down, rubbing his face.

'What a fucking mess. Jesus! Those absolute wankers.'

'Darling, what's going on?' Evelyn swivelled around in her chair to face him. 'What on earth's happened since your breakfast?'

Seb lifted his head and met her eyes. 'As soon as I waved off the journos I got pulled into a room by Carrie.'

Carrie was their in-house public relations manager. She was straight-talking and excellent at her job. Unfortunately, a large part of her role involved fighting fires. Evelyn assumed that, as usual, some tabloid would be taking issue with their food philosophies, their recipes, their science, their success... it was all fair game where the press was concerned.

'Right. And...?' she prompted.

He picked at a speck on his chinos. 'The *Daily Post* has

got hold of some pap shots of me. They're fairly... damning. And they're intent on publishing them. Carrie's on the phone with the editor now, trying to negotiate something.'

'What do you mean, they're damning?' Evelyn's throat went dry, and she felt a little dizzy. She had no idea where this was going. In her less secure moments, she sometimes wondered if there were other women. Seb was insanely attractive and very wealthy; he also travelled a lot. There were plenty of opportunities to cheat, if he was so inclined. And yet, despite the good-natured flirting (on his side) and overt interest (on the side of most women he met), Evelyn had never picked up any suspicious vibes when she saw him interacting with other women.

Seb looked up at her, reached over and took her hand. 'Ev, there's no easy way to say this. I just want you to know that I love you, and we're a team, right?' He gestured at the office. 'I mean, we're a fucking *dream* team. Don't forget that. You're my person.'

Evelyn nodded dumbly.

'Ev, the shots were taken in Soho. Outside—outside a gay club. They have footage of me with another guy, outside a gay club.'

What?

Evelyn shrank back in her chair. A gay club? 'What on earth were you doing in a gay club?' she asked stupidly. She was aware of a rising wave of nausea. She searched his dear, familiar face. 'Seb, I'm sorry, I don't understand...'

'Listen to me,' said Seb. 'This is not how we should be doing this. I hoped never to have this conversation with you, and thanks to those fucks at the *Post* I'm having to have it on the hoof, in our fucking *offices*, for Christ's sake. So I'm thinking out loud right now, but bear with me Ev. Listen.' He inhaled and exhaled deeply and rubbed the back of her hand with his thumb. 'You are my wife. You're my *life*. I love you. I made a vow, and I meant it. *But*. But, but, but. There is a part of me you've never seen, that I don't let anybody see, but it's stronger than I am and I can't defeat it completely. I've tried. I've tried for years and years, but I have needs. I have needs that don't fit with my carefully laid plans for my life, and so I keep them separate. I keep them secret and I just—I deal with them when I have to. Hence the photos, hence the club, hence the... guy.'

Evelyn felt as though her world was shattering, splintering into a million tiny fragments so that it looked nothing like her world of five minutes ago. She was aware that she was clinging to Seb's hand as if she were drowning and yet, this man whom she was treating as her rock, who was the axis around which her universe rotated, was in fact the very thing that was imploding before her eyes. He was the single source from which everything sprang—her happiness, her security, her identity, her *career*, for God's sake—and she didn't know him. She couldn't trust what she saw in front of her.

She had always prided herself on being fairly self-sufficient. She wasn't one of those codependent, needy, drippy wives. She was secure; she trusted her gut; she held firm opinions; when Seb travelled, she found the space to be quite delightful, actually. She had regular social outings with girlfriends. You had to be self-sufficient, really, when you had a famous husband. You had to get used to sharing him. But what she hadn't appreciated until now was how dependent all of this apparent *in*dependence was on the quiet, constant certainty that a happy marriage provided.

Their partnership underpinned everything else, and that foundation looked to be shifting by the second.

'Ok, so...' She tried to pull herself together, to think clearly. 'In no particular order, you're telling me that you're gay—or something, that you've been cheating on me—hang on, do I need to get *tested*?' She shrieked as she considered the last point. 'Wait.' She held her hand out as Seb opened his mouth to speak. 'I'm not done. So you have a secret life, I have no bloody idea who you are, really, and now a tabloid is threatening to blow your cover and ruin both our lives and everything we've worked so hard for—do I have this right?'

'I know how this looks, darling,' pleaded Seb. 'Christ, in black and white it sounds fucking awful. But you have to understand, I keep these parts of myself very, very compartmentalised. This is my real life, right here; this is what's important to me. You, Eddie, our beautiful home, our friends, this amazing company that we've built *together*, Ev. This is the life I chose, and dreamed of, and worked my arse off for. It's fucking amazing, and I love it.

'Except—inconveniently, my body seems to have other ideas. And try as I may, I can't ignore them, but I don't want to have them. I want to be the person you think I am, that everyone thinks I am, for fuck's sake. And honestly, the dishonesty and the lying and sneaking around makes me sick, but I do it so I can preserve this life with you. And it's been just about manageable—shitty but manageable—and now this fucking paper is just going to throw a huge fucking hand-grenade at our lives and treat us like tabloid fodder. I'm not having it, Ev. I won't let them do this to us.'

Evelyn thought she might throw up. 'I don't know what to say. What in God's name am I supposed to say to this? This isn't just your life Seb, it's my life too. You're so used to getting whatever you want that you thought you could just waltz into this marriage and take what you wanted from it, and then take whatever else you needed on the side. Life is not a bloody buffet, Seb. Where on *earth* did you get that level of entitlement from? Did it ever occur to you that I might quite like to have a straight husband? Seriously, that doesn't seem too much to ask, does it? *God*, your arrogance is just breathtaking. I feel so stupid.'

'Oh God, sweetheart. I'm so, so sorry. Shit. This has not been a cold-blooded deception, I promise. It's much more complicated than that. Shonda says I've been lying to myself—'

'Shonda?' Evelyn's head jerked up. 'Your therapist knows about this? Of course she bloody does!'

'It's the primary reason I got a therapist in the first place,' admitted Seb. 'She doesn't approve at all. She's been telling me for years that I need to embrace my truth, surrender, stop living a lie—her words—and to level with you.'

'So... you're gay? Shonda thinks you're actually gay—not bi, not confused?'

Seb squirmed. 'I really don't like labels, but yes. I'm gay. I've been sure of it since school. There's nothing I can do about how I'm wired, but there's a lot I can do about whether I act on it. That's where Shonda comes in. Her mandate has never been to help me decide if and when to come out; her mandate is to help me manage this without my brain exploding, because this is the life that I've chosen.'

He leaned forward. 'Ev, I did not get into this marriage as some kind of stop-gap or cover-up. I have always intended this to be for life. I married my soul-mate and my best friend —my very beautiful best friend.

'But, I have to admit, I've been finding it harder and harder to deal with it all over the last couple of years. I guess it's been the stress of growing the company, of having the investors breathing down our necks constantly, of having an increasingly high profile... plus, I always have guys hitting on me.'

This was true. Seb's fan-base included many gay men, something Evelyn had always found amusing—until now.

'So I guess I've been getting more and more stressed without having had an outlet for it...' he tailed off, seeing her face.

'How often do you cheat on me?'

Seb looked down. 'Probably once a fortnight.'

God. Once a fortnight! Evelyn's whole abdomen contracted in pain. She had a morbid urge to imagine her husband in the arms of another man, but she couldn't go there yet. 'Same guy or different guys?'

'Different guys.'

'Where?'

'Hotel rooms usually, and often abroad.'

'Nice,' said Evelyn. 'Really nice, Seb. This brings me back to my question: do I need to get tested?'

'No!' Seb looked horrified. 'I'm super, super careful, I promise, Ev. And I get tested regularly.'

'Does anyone else in the company know?'

'Only Carrie.'

Only Carrie. Evelyn let the words sink in. Right now Carrie was earning her stripes, negotiating with those sleazy journalists. She was their best bet at stopping what was, for now, a personal nightmare from going nuclear.

'Look,' said Seb. 'I can't even imagine how awful this must be for you. I've been blindsided by this, but you've been... well, I know you've had the rug pulled out from under you. I know this will be a long road for us and we need to talk about everything a lot more. But, right now the clock is ticking and we need to get Carrie in as soon as humanly possible to see if we can stop this thing from going public. It sounds awful to say, but at this very moment our marriage is not our biggest problem, it's this fucking tabloid, and the havoc it can wreak on the brand.'

At the mention of the brand, Evelyn nodded. 'Agreed, I guess. Let's call her in.'

~

CARRIE LOGAN KNOCKED and then entered the room. She was small, wiry and freckled, and was holding a bottle of vanilla vodka and two shot glasses. She took a look at Evelyn's face, put the glasses down and unscrewed the vodka.

'Evelyn. I'm so sorry that this conversation is necessary at what must be a very tough time for you.' She slid a full shot glass across the desk to Evelyn. 'Drink this.'

'But it's ten o'clock in the morning!' gasped Evelyn.

'I know. But you're in shock. Drink it. It'll take the edge off, I promise.' Carrie handed the other glass to Seb. They wordlessly downed their shots. *Jesus*. That was revolting. Even so, the liquid's blessed, numbing warmth spread through her body almost immediately. Wow. What a genius move by Carrie. Later on it would occur to her that Carrie had managed this whole situation brilliantly. Perhaps 'Handling Tabloid Bombshells Exposing Your Boss as Gay and Managing His Distraught Wife' should be a case-study for future PR staff recruitment drives. There weren't many more horrifying crises you could throw at your PR department, as far as she could tell.

Carrie pulled up a seat at the desk. 'So this is where we are. There's no way they'll let us buy the photos off them.

They're way too incendiary for that. We went through several *quid pro quo* options and there's only one that they'll agree to. But it's not a full win, I'm warning you.'

'What is it?' Seb asked confidently. 'Ev and I haven't had a chance to discuss it yet, but I'm sure we'd be happy to offer an exclusive, great access, maybe at home?'

'This is what I've secured for you.' Carrie leaned forward, hands clasped in front of her on the desk. 'You won't like it, but there's no other option, and it's a hell of a lot better than the alternative.

'They'll ditch the article *and* they'll hand the photos over to us to destroy or do with as we please. But, and it's a big but, they want a full exclusive interview and photo shoot at home with you both, in which you come out as gay, Seb. We can position you sympathetically and allow you to tell your story in your own words—they'll even give us sign-off on the article before it goes live.'

'FUCK! Fuck, fuck, fuck.' Seb put his head in his hands. Evelyn was frozen with horror in her seat. She couldn't believe that this was happening, that her husband of nine years was about to be outed as gay—indeed, she couldn't believe that he even was gay.

'I know it sounds hideous, but this is a good deal, guys,' said Carrie calmly. 'We get in front of the story; you can position it with whatever back-story you want, Seb, in terms of your inner turmoil or whatever else you want to talk about. This needn't be some seedy exposé; you'll be seen as a well-loved household figure who's been brave enough to come forward and live his truth. You can both present a united front—if that's the way you're comfortable going. You don't have to be on the defensive. You're in charge—both of you—and it's your story to tell. You can be unapologetic.

'If we get this right, this revelation doesn't have to

damage your brand. It can even be a positive. You've got a strong gay fan-base and, generally, the public is supportive of stuff like this. We're all aware of how many men of your generation have had to make tough choices in life. Society was a hell of a lot less supportive of people coming out twenty years ago than it is now. This does not need to be a death-knell for you. But, if you let them publish the pap photos then it will be a fucking shit-show for you both and for Eddie.'

She sat back and looked at them both, gauging their reactions.

'What do you reckon, Ev?' asked Seb tentatively. 'It doesn't sound like we have much choice, does it?'

'No,' said Ev, blowing her nose. 'It doesn't. They have us backed into a corner and it's a horrifying situation to face, but I appreciate that you've done a superb job by securing this deal, Carrie. Thank you.' She smiled gratefully at Carrie.

'What's the timing on this?' asked Seb. 'I mean, there's so much to sort out just between the two of us, before we even come up with an official 'message' of sorts on this.'

'They want the article out by next Friday latest, so you've got a week till it hits.' Carrie pulled out her phone. 'They can't do much over the long weekend so I propose we push for Wednesday for the interview and shoot. We'll keep the shoot quick; I don't see any good reason to include Eddie, but that's your call.'

Seb and Evelyn glanced at each other, horrified. Eddie. Trying to protect their little son from the upcoming media maelstrom would involve a whole other level of effort and heartache.

'No,' Evelyn shook her head quickly. 'They don't get their hands on Eddie at all. He's on half-term next week, but we'll get him out of the house for it—I can sign him up for school camp.'

'Ok then,' Carrie confirmed. 'Wednesday gives them twenty-four hours to polish it up for publication. It also gives you two time beforehand to talk, to soul-search, to work out what your next steps will be as a couple. I'm around to help you get the messaging straight on this and do interview prep whenever you're ready to start that part. And we'll also need to make a game-plan for the media frenzy once the article goes live.

'I suggest we keep this between the three of us for now and we can brief anyone else internally—plus your investors—on a need-to-know basis nearer the time. *Food* magazine will go absolutely ape-shit; you're on their cover on every supermarket shelf in the country playing happy families as we speak, but that's the least of our worries.

'Seb, it looks like you're due to be in Italy next week, Thursday till Sunday, for that inspiration trip. If I were you, I'd go ahead with it; it gets you out of the country and far away from those paps, and it will look like it's business as usual for the company.'

She held up the vodka bottle. 'Be strong, people. This is happening. Anyone need another shot?'

3

The meeting over, Evelyn booted Seb out of her office and then headed home in the welcome anonymity of a black cab. She needed to get the hell away from him so she could think straight. She exhaled as she stepped into her magnificent hallway and shut the heavy front door against the outside world. The sheer scale of the space, with its immense door-frames, sweeping staircase and monochrome palate, had a grounding effect on her. She was home; she was safe.

She felt exhausted and nauseous. It occurred to her that today might not be the best day to indulge in intermittent fasting, and besides, doing a shot of vodka mid-morning wasn't exactly a textbook approach. She grabbed a hard-boiled egg and an avocado from the cavernous fridge and devoured them both with a few raspberries, then spread some almond butter on lentil crackers and scoffed those. Better. She filled a large jug with water and, running on autopilot, added ice, some sprigs of mint, and long ribbons of cucumber. She carried the jug out to the garden with a glass and her phone, and collapsed onto one of the generously cushioned teak sun-loungers that lined the limestone patio, kicking off her sandals.

The garden was an oasis, and very large for central London, though Seb and Evelyn had always laughed about the fact that you could spend eight figures on a Holland Park villa and feel grateful for a patch of grass that wouldn't look out of place on your average suburban semi-detached house. Even so, it was stunning. The spacious patio made way for a raised lawn bordered with deep flower beds and dotted with mature, gnarled olive trees. Wisteria and jasmine covered the walls of the garden. The wisteria blooms had sadly gone—wisteria bloomed early in London —but the jasmine would be in flower soon. Evelyn's favourite thing to do in June was to come straight out to the garden first thing in the morning and inhale the heady scent of jasmine as she did her yoga and meditation practice outside.

Back in the painful present moment, she sighed and unlocked her phone. There was only one person to call about this utter disaster—Jess. First, she, Seb and Eddie were supposed to be heading to Kent in a few hours. Second, Jess was Evelyn's oldest friend and biggest cheerleader. Third, Jess was gay, and Evelyn was desperate to know if she'd had unvoiced suspicions about Seb's sexuality.

She hit Jess' number.

'Hello my lovely!' enthused Jess. At the sound of her friend's warm, familiar voice, Evelyn's eyes filled, and she choked up.

'Oh Jess! Something awful has happened—shit. Jess, I don't know what to do.'

'Evie, what the fuck is wrong?' Evelyn didn't know anyone who used a greater density of swear-words in their everyday speech than Jess, a legacy of her years on a trading floor. 'Talk to me. What is it?'

'It's Seb.'

'Is he ok? Is he ill?'

'He's gay.'

'What the fuck? What the actual fuck? Seb's no more gay than I am straight. Where did you get that idea from?'

'It's true, Jess. He told me himself. Not voluntarily, of course. A tabloid's got hold of some grubby little shots of him outside some—some gay bar, or club, or something, in Soho, with a guy. A guy, Jess! And they're threatening to publish them, unless he agrees to come out exclusively to them next Friday.'

She waited for a stream of obscenities. None was forthcoming.

'Jess? Are you there?'

'Fuck.' Jess muttered under her breath. 'Evie, I did *not* see this coming. Oh my poor angel, I am devastated for you. Devastated. That fucking prick. Jesus. This—*this*—is why I don't do men anymore. For fuck's sake. What else do you know?'

Evelyn tried to think. 'He admitted he's gay, not bi or whatever. He's been seeing a shrink for years about it, apparently. He gave me a spiel about how it was a part of him he didn't want to accept and that Eddie and me were his proper life and his being gay is something he just deals with on the side. But he said it's been getting worse, getting harder.

'Um—he said he, you know, sleeps with other men every couple of weeks. Apparently it's something he 'needs' to do to handle the stress of it all. He said he's careful, and he loves me, and that our marriage is not a sham.'

'Well, I am fucking livid,' breathed Jess. 'You poor little lamb. What are you going to do? Do you want me to come up to London—I can get in the car right now? I can be there in an hour, and then I can fucking strangle him for you.'

'No, no, thanks sweets,' Evelyn managed a weak laugh. 'I'm supposed to be seeing you in a few hours, anyway. I don't know what to do about the weekend…'

'Do whatever you want to do. Do you want to ditch the entire trip? Or come down anyway, and we can keep Eddie entertained while you talk things through with Seb? Or you can tell him to go fuck himself, and you and Eddie escape down here for a couple of nights? It might—it might give you some breathing space?'

'Actually, yes.' Evelyn sat up straighter. 'Yeah, I think I need to get away from him. I just need not to see that bloody man for a day or two. And I've been looking forward to getting down to Kent so much. I need to get out of this place. Can Eddie and I come down anyway, for a night or two? I probably should get back on Sunday to deal with this tabloid situation—I'll fill you in on that later. But yes, thank you sweets. Count us in.'

'Excellent! Oh, I can't wait to have you down here, my angel. Are you in a fit state to drive?'

'Yep, definitely. A drive will do me good.' Evelyn loved driving; she found it almost meditative. Notwithstanding that she'd be hitting the M25 on a Friday afternoon before a bank holiday weekend, she relished the chance to get behind the wheel.

'Ok then. That's sorted. Why don't you go straight to the cottage and dump your bags when you get there? It's number eight. I'll get housekeeping to leave it open for you so you needn't face Reception. Then come over and we'll get stuck into the rosé. Ooh, Zoe and I will cook you up a feast.

'You know what you need, my girl? Carbs. You need a carb-fest. When was the last time you had a potato? I bet it's been fucking months. Carbs, a truck-load of rosé, and we'll put the world to rights while we feast. Can't wait to see you, my darling. I look forward to seeing that bony little arse of yours later.'

ACCORDINGLY, Evelyn found herself driving out of London that afternoon. She'd spent the rest of the day packing, avoiding Seb's calls, and responding to work emails with the bare minimum required of her.

When she'd picked Eddie up from school she'd armoured up with her biggest, darkest sunglasses. Aside from being accosted by one of the pushier mothers, a high-maintenance, Gucci-clad Italian called Chiara who was hoping that Evelyn and Seb could attend (and donate to) her upcoming charity event, she emerged relatively unscathed with Eddie in tow. She'd worried that her son might pick up on her tear-stained face and what felt like her overt fragility, only to be reminded that eight-year-old boys generally had the emotional intelligence of an amoeba, especially after a full week of school.

'How was school, darling?' she'd asked him.

'Fine,' he'd mumbled. 'What's for snack?'

And thus, she found herself in the car, Eddie glued to an Avengers movie on his iPad in the back, making decent headway down the M3 and around the M25. She'd selected a relaxing piano playlist on Spotify and the tranquil music filled the car, soothing her frazzled nerves. She shifted in her seat. She loved driving the Range Rover. Seb had a weakness for sports cars, particularly Jaguars and Aston Martins, but she hated being so low to the ground; it made her feel unsafe. The powerful Range Rover gave her a great vantage-point, and she felt wonderfully cocooned in its cream leather interior.

It had upset Seb to hear that she was going ahead with the Kent trip, but that he was not welcome to tag along. Evelyn didn't care. Quite frankly, with a decade of infidelity and lies under his belt, he could cut her some slack. She wasn't sure how she was feeling, or indeed how she should feel. She guessed that she was probably in shock.

She couldn't quite believe that what Seb had told her was true; she couldn't really equate his confessions of gay trysts in exotic hotels with the husband she knew, and loved, and slept next to. The entire thing was almost laughable. It sounded like a bad, far-fetched novel. She imagined Seb's mother, Adelaide, who was not the kind of woman one messed with, tutting and waving her hand dismissively and telling him, 'Oh don't be *silly*, darling. Of course you're not gay! Now run along and give Evelyn a nice kiss and stop making such a fuss.' Yikes. She felt almost sorry for Seb. That was not a call he'd be looking forward to.

And the news had shocked even Jess! If Seb hadn't even made it onto a lesbian's gaydar, how could he really be gay? Hmm. She wondered if that was why Seb avoided spending time with Jess and Zoe. Perhaps he thought that they'd pick up the scent, or perhaps it was just too painful, too close to home—a reminder of the wonderful happiness that they'd found by being true to themselves. He must have felt as though he was on the outside, looking in at what he could have had.

Her heart twisted. Seb had told her he'd spent the last few years 'managing' his conflict. He'd essentially made a Faustian pact with himself to choose societal acceptance. He'd built a wildly successful personal brand based on what he perceived as 'normal'—white, straight, nice wife, cute kid

—over what his heart had told him to be true. She wondered, fleetingly, what it must have been like for him, then dismissed the thought. Nope. She wasn't ready to feel sorry for him just yet. She had to put her own oxygen-mask on first.

M25 AND M20 COMPLETED, Evelyn reached the B-roads. The countryside of Kent's Bourne Valley came into focus as she drove down enchanting lanes that were considerably narrower than in the winter months, groaning as the roadside hedgerows were with an abundance of cow-parsley, forget-me-nots and hawthorn. She could see gorse in the fields and she slowed, lowering her window. God, she loved the smell of gorse. The intoxicating, coconut scent transported her straight back to her childhood nearby, though she remembered her mother telling her once that some people didn't experience the smell of gorse that strongly, while others found it pungent. She was thankful to be in the latter category. How quirky nature was.

Despite herself, a slight smile came to her lips. It was impossible not to feel affected by this bounteous, fragrant countryside. She felt as though their car was nestled in a giant, verdant womb. Trees created a canopy overhead, and the early evening sunlight strobed through the branches as they passed. The birds were singing, and the light illuminated the dancing swarms of midges delightfully. She was glad they'd come, and equally glad that she'd left her gay husband at home. She needed this reprieve. She glanced in the rear-view mirror at Eddie, still engrossed in his movie. The little man would have a difficult few weeks ahead, and this weekend would hopefully do him the world of good.

It was five-thirty when she pulled into the entrance to Sorrel Farm—they had made good time for a Friday—and Evelyn felt a familiar rush of appreciation for the magic that Jess and Zoe had created. A board read *Welcome to Sorrel Farm. Celebrate the Seasons.* They passed the enchanting gate-lodge and drove slowly down a long, tree-lined driveway. Evelyn ignored the *Reception* sign-post and instead followed the one marked *Cottages.* She absorbed the gentle ambience of the place—the couples meandering to the Oast House for a sun-downer, some guests picking their way back from the walled garden's freshwater pool in fluffy white Sorrel Farm robes and flip-flops, the Farm Shop, and the delightful wheelbarrows overflowing with wild English flowers.

She pulled up in a parking bay marked *Cottage Guests Only* and turned off the ignition. Eddie looked up, bewildered.

'Are we here, Mummy?'

'Yes honey, we're here,' she told him fondly.

'*Yippee!*' Eddie pulled off his headphones and unbuckled his seatbelt, opening his door and bounding down from the car. 'We're here!'

Evelyn beckoned to him and strolled over to the stone cottages. They were utterly charming, old farm-workers' dwellings clad with rambling roses and lichen-covered, russet roof-tiles. Each cottage had a small front lawn edged with lavender flowerbeds, a gravel pathway, and a duck-egg blue front door.

She tried the door handle; unlocked, as good old Jess had promised. Inside, the cottage was cool despite the evening light streaming through the back of the building. The spacious ground floor was entirely open-plan, laid with blond wood floorboards. Plump armchairs and a sofa surrounded the wood-burning stove, with neutral throws and cushions strewn over them. There was a tiny and delightful kitchenette and breakfast bar, all painted in oatmeal eggshell. A cellophane-wrapped pile of cookies and a bottle of wine stood on the rough-hewn kitchen table.

'Cookies!' Eddie cried and started to feverishly untie the bag. He grabbed one—the poor child was probably famished—and ran upstairs to explore. Evelyn looked around. It was perfect.

Right, she thought. Better get the bags in from the car. It was most definitely wine o'clock.

4

Evelyn and Eddie walked the short distance to Jess and Zoe's place hand-in-hand. She inhaled the heady scent of roses and white lilac as they strolled. When Jess had taken over the running of the farm from her parents, she, Zoe and the kids had moved into the original farmhouse and had done an incredible job of renovating it.

Evelyn had fond memories of her countless visits to the farmhouse during her school years, of standing by the Aga, scoffing crumpets after she and Jess been to the local pub. Like Jess' parents themselves, the house had always been cosy and welcoming, with endless dogs on the sagging, threadbare sofas. Now it was almost unrecognisable. Nothing sagged these days. The brick had been sandblasted, the sash windows restored, and—Evelyn's favourite part—the back of the ground floor had been replaced with a vast glass box, a garden room whose view over the Bourne Valley was hard to match.

Jess and Zoe had two children, and like everything else that they'd accomplished together, Evelyn was full of admiration for how they'd built their family. They'd each carried one child from the same sperm donor. Michael, aged fourteen, was a solid, good-natured, blond kid who was just like Jess. Mia, eleven, was tall and willowy like Zoe, with olive-coloured skin and the most incredible pale hazel eyes. Like her mother, she was a gentle, reflective little thing and would be a real beauty. The best bit, as far as Evelyn was concerned, was that they were brilliant with Eddie—close enough to him in age to take pleasure in playing with him, and old enough to look after him. Having the Augustin-Holmes kids around meant that Eddie would get a real taste of freedom on the farm this weekend.

Evelyn knocked on the door and Jess opened it, enveloping both Evelyn and Eddie in a swirl of blond curls and the scent of lavender.

'My favourite people!' she cried. 'It is so good to see your faces! Come in, come in!'

'Hello, you,' said Evelyn, hugging her gratefully. 'It's very good to be here.'

The farmhouse had been reconfigured so that the hall led straight through to the garden room at the back of the house and the terrace beyond. Evelyn marvelled at the sight ahead: a perfectly framed slice of the heaven that awaited them outside. As they walked out onto the terrace, she couldn't help but gasp. Her manicured London garden was one thing, but this was truly nature at its most restorative. Fruit trees dotted the sloping lawn, and clematis and jasmine covered an ancient wall along the right-hand side. The creepers concealed a door providing direct access to the resort's walled garden next door. Straight ahead, the lawn ran down to an old ha-ha, affording an unbroken view across to the fields beyond. It was a magical vista, especially in the hazy evening sunshine that cast long shadows across the grass.

Zoe rose from the garden table and greeted Evelyn with a kiss on each cheek. She tousled Eddie's hair.

'I'm so pleased you could make it, Evie,' she said warmly. 'Eddie, Mike and Mia are in the family room if you want to go find them? Then you can all run over to the walled garden to grab your pizzas from the pizza oven—Alberto is making them specially for you.'

'Awesome!' shouted Eddie as he scampered back into the house.

Jess put her arms around Evelyn and hugged her hard. 'How are you doing, my dear?' she asked, pulling back to study Evelyn's face.

'Ugh, I don't know.' This had been precisely the right course of action—to come down here, get away from Seb and London, and collapse into the comforting arms of her oldest friend. 'I'm exhausted, actually; it's been a long day. This morning feels like a million years ago.'

'You must be completely drained,' said Jess. 'Have a sit-down, and let's get you a drink.' She pulled a bottle of palest pink rosé out of the wine-cooler and poured Evelyn an enormous glass. 'Ice? There's not much in the world that Whispering Angel can't fix, so get that down you. How is Eddie doing—what did you tell him?'

'I just told him that Daddy had come down with a cold and was going to stay in London and have a rest.' Evelyn shrugged and took a sip of her rosé. Christ, that was delicious. She took a decent gulp. 'He didn't seem that interested. He was far more focused on seeing Mike and Mia, and he's desperate to go on a tractor this weekend.'

'Bless him; we can most definitely arrange that,' said Jess. 'We'll do supper shortly if that works; Zoe's been cooking up a feast. We thought you'd be pretty knackered and hungry. Meanwhile, get stuck into some of this.' She gestured towards a huge blue-and-white platter of crudites: long, rosy French radishes with white tips, tapered carrots with feathery tops still attached and long wedges of cucumber surrounding a bowl of creamy houmous. There was also a wooden dish of almonds, roasted with rosemary. It looked delicious; in fact, the entire table looked spectacular. Chunky white plates jostled for position on the wooden table-top with blue-and-white linen napkins, rosemary in little clay pots, thick, hand-blown glass tumblers, and jam-jars full of white flowers and greenery. The overall effect was utterly charming.

'Zoe, you've surpassed yourself already and I haven't even tried the food yet,' said Evelyn. 'Seriously, ladies, just... thank you. Thank you for all this—what an antidote it is to the day I've had.'

'It's our pleasure, Evie,' smiled Zoe. 'Tuck in, as you Brits say. Excuse me, *mes filles*, while I go rest the chicken.'

She rose in her balletic way and kissed Jess on the top of her head before heading back into the house. Jess watched her wife affectionately, then turned her gaze back to Evelyn.

'Right, my dear. Drink up and tell me everything. Where the fuck do we start?'

'Well, it's funny,' began Evelyn, taking another large mouthful of wine. It was slipping down like water. 'I've had such an unbelievable bombshell thrown at me today, and yet I don't really know how it will change things for us. It's not as though Seb's announced he's walking out on me. From what he said it sounds like he's very committed to our marriage. I mean, it's almost clinical the way he talked about the choices he's made in his life, as if settling down with me was part of a grand plan he had.'

'I never had Seb down as an idiot, but he's a fucking moron if he thinks his sexuality is some sort of lifestyle choice,' retorted Jess, helping herself to a radish liberally adorned with houmous. 'I'm aware that Seb Macleod has always got everything he ever wanted, with a big fucking bow on it, so it figures that he thought he could control *who* he wanted too, but guess what? He can't. Honestly, the level of delusion is just staggering, for fuck's sake. So what happens now—with his coming out, I mean?'

'The coming out has to happen,' explained Evelyn, crunching on a delicious almond. 'The *Post* has us over a barrel. Either he comes out to them or they publish these photos. They're going to come and interview us both next Wednesday. We haven't even talked about it yet—not properly. We have five days to work out what to do and what to say.' Her head reeled just thinking of it. Five days to strategise on her marriage and package it neatly for the media. She took another gulp of wine.

'Hmm,' said Jess. 'What are you thinking, angel? Have you any idea what *you* want? Do you want out?'

'Oh God, I don't know!' cried Evelyn. 'It's so weird, because he's still my husband—he's still the same person who I love, who I fancy—I can't just turn that off.'

'Of course you can't.'

'But, it's as if I've just found out none of it was real. It's not as though he cheated on me with some girl and we can go to marriage counselling and maybe move on. I mean, he's *gay*, for God's sake! I can't just ignore that, can I? It's a pretty fundamental problem. But then again, we have a strong marriage. We're a brilliant team. We're *great* together at work; we riff off each other; we're so well-matched in that regard and for me, that's always been an enormous part of our chemistry. Also, you know how important the company is to both of us; there's no way we're about to throw all our hard work down the drain.

'And we're parents—that's a pretty big bond right there. He's a great dad; I love seeing him and Eddie together. In all those ways, it's fantastic. Is that something worth trying to save? I don't know. I'd actually say that on most fronts we have a fairly happy marriage compared to many people, all things considered—'

She broke off as Zoe came back to the table, bearing a plump, uniformly golden chicken.

'Fuck me, that looks good,' beamed Jess, springing up to take the platter. '*Thank you*, darling.'

THE MEAL WAS INCREDIBLE. Zoe had served up the chicken with mounds of buttered and minted new potatoes, and peas picked that morning from the walled garden. Evelyn surprised herself with her appetite and continued to accept the healthy refills of rosé that Jess administered. As they put their knives and forks together, Jess leaned forward.

'Right, Evie. You've had enough wine to handle this question. For the love of God, give me some dirt on your sex life with Seb. Was there no clue there that he was gay?'

Evelyn squirmed. She knew it was a fair question, and that Jess wouldn't be afraid to ask it. Back in their university days they had both regaled each other with every detail of their sex lives, laughing hysterically at the expense of some poor guy when they met up in the holidays and filled each other in on the previous term's exploits over Bacardi and Cokes.

But since they'd got older and settled into serious relationships and marriage, it had never been as appropriate to talk about what went on in the bedroom. When you had a significant other, sex was between you and them. Baring those intimacies, even to your closest friends, felt like a betrayal. Evelyn had pushed Jess on how the machinations of lesbian sex worked in general—it was a fascinating subject, after all—and Jess had enthusiastically obliged with plenty of detail. But the days of dissecting their sexual experiences were long gone.

Evelyn found it a fairly horrifying topic to get into, particularly as she felt very defensive. It would be the first question that everyone had after Seb came out. How on *earth* had the poor wife not known that something was up? On top of being devastated, she felt stupid. She thought of the infinite trust that she'd placed in her husband as he'd moved inside her on so many occasions over the years, trust that he was exactly where he wanted to be at those moments, and that she could be at her most vulnerable with him. Surely true intimacy meant laying all your cards on the table. She'd laid hers gladly, only to find that he'd been playing most of his close to his chest all this time.

If she'd had to describe their sex life before now, she would have said it was perfectly fine, nice, even. It was certainly sporadic—once every couple of months, at the most—and while deep-down she suspected that that was far less regular than in most of her friends' marriages, it was something she tried not to think about. They were both busy, knackered, working parents after all. It was true that sex had become less and less frequent over the years, and that it tended to be loving and comforting rather than passionately frenzied, but surely no married couples with kids had the energy to tear each other's clothes off regularly?

It was also true that Seb never went down on her. She

felt sure that if she admitted that to Jess and Zoe, they would be absolutely horrified. Oral sex was presumably fairly fundamental if you were a lesbian. But it wasn't something she'd ever had the guts to bring up with him, and in any case, he was conscientious and attentive in other ways in bed, and so she had no complaints, really.

But now she was mortified. Had Seb been going through the motions all these years? Or worse, had he been secretly repulsed by having to make love to a person he wasn't physically attracted to? Had he viewed sex with his wife as a necessary evil, a task to be ticked off the list every few weeks so she never suspected his secret, an unappetising price to pay for the life that he had so carefully crafted for himself?

She had so many questions for Seb, and yet she doubted she wanted to know the answers to any of them.

5

Evelyn woke with a jolt at five-thirty the next morning. She'd slept through the night, the bottle of wine she'd drunk having provided the desired oblivion. Now, her mouth tasted acidic and her entire body felt heavy, but she knew that going back to sleep would be impossible when she felt this rough.

She was reluctant to face the day. Her new reality had hit her as soon as she'd regained consciousness, her brain instantly downloading all the salient facts for her with what seemed unnecessary efficiency. Perhaps this was why other people thought her early morning routine was crazy. Perhaps most people, who had actual problems, were as loath to face the day ahead as she now was.

Nevertheless, on the count of three she yanked back the bedclothes and padded into the bathroom to brush her teeth and splash some water on her face. She badly needed something to alkalise her body. She and Seb were advocates of an alkaline diet, and they'd recently partnered with a supplement brand to launch a nifty green effervescent tablet packed full of premium ingredients. She might need a whole tube of those tablets today, post her bottle of rosé and two slices of Zoe's rhubarb *galette* with *crème anglaise*.

She was furious with herself for folding so easily as soon as things got tough. Granted, the dessert had been delectable, and she'd been aware that it would be bad form to decline food that someone had cooked with love especially for you—always accept a gift in the spirit in which it's given, and all that. And the rosé had done its job of providing a pleasurable numbing effect. But still. She hadn't made it this far in life without putting strict protocols in place, and none of those protocols involved vodka shots at ten in the morning or mindlessly consuming sugar-laden drinks or desserts. She could tell herself that she deserved to let her hair down a little after the shock she'd had, but it wouldn't be true. Her discipline was her friend; it was her greatest super-power.

When she stayed inside her boundaries and maintained her focus, she could achieve anything. She'd proven that time and time again, just as her parents had provided her with countless examples of the kind of mediocrity that life accorded you when you let things slip. Focus was, to Evelyn, a mechanism that let her rise above the humdrum distractions and temptations of daily life. When she focused, all the noise fell away, and it was just her, her goal, and what felt like a straight path ahead. It was amazing how straightforward it was, really. Of course, it was the execution that was difficult, the ability to stay on track. That was where most people fell down.

Downstairs, the early morning light was pouring through the front windows. Well, at least Seb had had the decency to get outed at a pleasant time of year. It would be a hell of a lot more depressing to be confronted with her current situation in mid-January. Evelyn dissolved her supplement in a small glass of water and necked the contents. That was better.

The house was quiet. Eddie had insisted on sleeping over at Jess' and was hopefully still sound asleep on Mike's trundle-bed. Evelyn cast her eye around the large living-space. She felt like crap, but she was itchy. It certainly wasn't a morning for interval training, but perhaps some restorative yoga would do the trick, help get her back on track. She'd noticed yesterday that a cappuccino-coloured yoga mat—very on-brand for the resort—had been thoughtfully placed next to the TV. She ran back upstairs, swapped her fluffy robe for a black crop-top and some mesh-panelled yoga pants, and took her mat out onto the sunlit front lawn.

Outside, the resort was tranquil. Her fellow guests slept, but nature was already building up for another busy day. Flies darted around, some bees pottered industriously, and a few white butterflies flitted among the flowerbeds.

Evelyn rolled the mat out on her front lawn so it faced the sun, and stood at the top of the mat, hands in prayer position. She shut her eyes, willing herself to ground into the earth. *Forget the gay husband, the turmoil, the uncertainty, the anxiety, and the hangover*, she told herself. *Focus on the present moment, on the sun on your face, on growing taller, on slowing your breath, on finding your centre. Focus on grounding down through all four corners of your feet, on the smell of lilac, on the warm certainty of your palms as they meet.* She cast her arms out wide to bring them skyward and began her sun-salutations.

Evelyn settled into a vinyasa flow that comforted and challenged her in equal measure. It was a relief to find her body responding to the familiar poses, to feel that reassuring strength in her delts and lats, her quads and abs. She carefully lifted herself out of her dolphin pose into a forearm headstand, one leg at a time. Finding her balance, she clasped her hands together, settled into the posture and closed her eyes, focusing on her controlled *ujayii* breathing.

Suddenly, a scuffling sound shattered her precious moment of serenity. Before she could react, her senses were assaulted by the smell, feeling and taste of a dog exuberantly licking her face.

'Charlie!' she heard a man's voice hiss in panic. '*Charlie*. Come here!'

Evelyn's eyes shot open. All she could see was black fur, far too close, and an upside-down tongue attempting to devour her mouth and face.

'Mmm!' she squeaked—it was the only sound she could make with her lips clamped firmly shut. She hastily came down from her headstand, far less gracefully than she'd entered it, and clambered to her feet to escape the onslaught, wiping her wet mouth with the back of her hand. A glossy black spaniel, leggy but presumably still a puppy (Evelyn didn't know too much about dogs), was jumping up at her, tongue hanging out comically to one side, tail wagging enthusiastically, pawing at her yoga pants.

The puppy's presumed owner came into view: a tall, well-built man, dressed in wellies, jeans and a checked shirt, sleeves rolled up, under a Sorrel Farm-branded gilet.

'Oh my God, I'm so sorry!' he gasped, trying to keep his voice down given the early hour. 'Charlie. *Charlie*. Come here.' He rummaged in his pocket and pulled out a doggie treat, offering it out. 'Come here. Good boy, good boy.'

Charlie abandoned Evelyn and hot-footed it over to his owner, gobbling up the treat in a flash before bounding back to her. This time she was prepared and kept her face at a safe distance as she reached down to stroke him.

'I really am dreadfully sorry,' the man continued. 'He's only six months old and still very excitable. I'm afraid if he spots a face at ground-level it's like a red rag to a bull.'

He grinned, and his hazel eyes crinkled. 'Clearly we have a lot more work to do on the training front. I always try to take him with me on my morning rounds; it's usually quiet enough at this hour that we can avoid violating any of the guests unnecessarily.'

Evelyn felt slightly light-headed after coming down so quickly from her headstand. Her face must still be very red from the blood-rush.

'It's totally fine,' she assured him, caressing Charlie's silky head. 'He's very cute. And I'm sure he's not used to finding strange women upside-down on his morning walk.'

'It looked very impressive,' said the man, 'and you seemed quite peaceful there—till we came along, at any rate. It's a far more Zen start to the day than mine has been, fondling cow's udders and such. I'm sorry we disturbed you.'

He raked a hand through his short, greying hair and Evelyn observed idly that his forearms were deeply tanned, and very muscular. He really was very attractive.

'Honestly, it's quite alright,' she insisted. 'It's flattering to be greeted so enthusiastically.' She suddenly felt exposed in her crop top, and folded her arms over her chest.

'Spaniels are definitely a giant ego-boost,' he agreed. 'Well, I'll get him out of your hair. Come along, you little mutt. Good morning to you.'

He nodded smilingly at Evelyn and strolled off, Charlie falling eagerly into line by his side.

'Have a good morning,' echoed Evelyn. She watched them walk a little way, enjoying the artfully lit view of man and dog in the hazy morning sunlight. She settled into a forward-fold. He really had had very nice forearms, very *masculine* forearms. Pull yourself together, she told herself. Your husband tells you he's gay, and twenty-four hours later you're lusting over a manly farmer. You don't need a therapist to work out what's going on there. Get a grip, for God's sake. And exhale.

6

The Oast House at breakfast-time was quieter than Evelyn had expected to find it on a bank-holiday weekend. She explained to the woman on the door that she was meeting Jess, and chose a small table by the French doors, gathering up the skirts of her floaty Chloé maxi-dress before she sat. She looked around, drinking in the scene before her.

The building had once been a traditional Kentish oast house, its conical roofs the homes of kilns used to dry out hops. Jess and Zoe had sensitively transformed and extended it, using original, locally sourced bricks. The result was a wonderful space that formed the hub of the Sorrel Farm resort. It boasted vaulted ceilings high enough to accommodate a mezzanine level at each end, where enormous sofas enticed guests to kick back and escape the outside world. On the ground level was an open kitchen at one end and a semi-circular bar at the other. Between the two, tables of various sizes punctuated the room. Small posies of wild flowers, in enamel jugs or old apothecary bottles, adorned each table.

Evelyn still felt out of sorts, although the yoga and a long, hot shower had done her some good. It wasn't just her hangover that was bothering her, but a sinking sensation in her stomach every time she considered the predicament she and Seb were in. The primal, ancient part of her craved her husband and wanted him sitting across from her, as they'd planned. She should have been settling in for breakfast with him right now, enjoying his handsome face, his witty conversation, and the slight stir that his arrival anywhere tended to cause.

She couldn't deny that seeing other people's reactions to him gave her a boost. She'd always felt so proud, so *validated*, to be his chosen partner. Well, she had less than a week left of that before the *Post* pulled the plug on life as they knew it. She supposed they wouldn't be able to show their faces at all in public once the news hit and the paps hounded them.

She would have to steel herself for looks of a different kind: sneering, vicious, pitying, curious—all of which would be as bad as each other. Oh, it was infuriating, galling, that the man who'd led them to the heights of success and the most elite circles of London society was responsible for sabotaging all of their achievements, unconsciously or not.

Evelyn watched Jess enter through the far door, by the bar, and weave through the room. She was in conversation with someone. Evelyn recognised him, to her surprise, as the man whose puppy had accosted her earlier. Jess spotted her and waved, and as they drew nearer, he gave a slight jolt of recognition.

'Hello, angel,' said Jess as they reached the table. 'Meet Angus Rutherford, our farm manager—Angus, this is my gorgeous friend, Evelyn Macleod.'

Evelyn rolled her eyes at Jess' typical hyperbole and held up her hand in greeting.

'Hi Angus. Good to meet you properly. We've already met,' she told Jess.

'I'm afraid Charlie launched himself on Evelyn earlier this morning,' explained Angus. 'He took a liking to her as she was trying to do some yoga.' He gave her another of his crinkly smiles.

'Oh, bless him!' said Jess. 'He's such an affectionate little guy.'

'He's very keen on Jess too,' Angus offered. 'I'm sure it's nothing to do with the bits of bacon she's always sneaking him.'

'He's a cheap date; what can I say?' Jess pulled back a chair and sat down opposite Evelyn. 'Angus is on his way to a team meeting upstairs, but we were just talking about you, actually. I mentioned we had a VIP guest staying—Eddie, not you—who was desperate for a tractor ride. Angus is happy to take you guys out later this morning. There's no one better to talk you through how the farm works.'

'I beg to differ, Jess,' protested Angus. 'You're the expert. But yes, I'd be delighted to take you and your son out. It would be in the Land Rover, I'm afraid—it's a little more nimble than the tractor—but he can have a clamber around some farm machinery while we're doing the rounds.'

'That would be amazing, thank you!' exclaimed Evelyn. 'Eddie will be so excited. Did he get any sleep last night, Jess?'

'They were still giggling when Zoe and I turned in, but he's very perky this morning,' said Jess. 'Oh, to have youth on your side. I left them eating toast in front of the TV. Aurelie, our *au pair*, is watching them as Zoe's been in the kitchen since early doors.' She gestured over to the open-plan kitchen at the far end of the room. 'What time suits you for the grand tour, Angus?'

He checked his watch. 'Does ten o'clock work? I can meet you outside the Oast House?'

'That's perfect, thanks so much,' Evelyn said. 'It really is very kind of you.'

'No bother at all. See you in a bit.'

'You'll be in expert hands with Angus,' said Jess, as he walked away. 'He's a fucking rockstar. I defy you not to be obsessed by soil by the time he's done; he makes the subject fascinating. I kid you not. Right, let's grab some breakfast and we can have a good chat.'

They made their way to the kitchen, in front of which was an enormous old banqueting table, groaning with food. The breakfast buffet was beautifully arranged on vintage platters and chunky wooden boards crafted from highly polished cross-sections of tree-trunk. Evelyn took a plate and made her way slowly down the table, her eyes lingering on vast bowls of creamy Greek yoghurt and what must be homemade granola, whose thick clusters of honeyed oats were piled high. She hurried on before temptation could strike, also attempting to ignore the mounds of rustic sourdough loaves, fresh croissants and baguettes. When you were gluten-free, hotel breakfast buffets were an absolute minefield.

Behind the savoury end of the table, she spotted Zoe and blew her a kiss.

'*Bon matin, ma chérie,*' called Zoe. 'How are you doing this morning? Can I tempt you with an omelette? Ramit here can make you one to order. I recommend adding asparagus and herbs fresh from the garden. We'll bring it over to you.'

Settled back at the table, Jess and Evelyn fell into conversation.

'How are you feeling about things this morning?' probed Jess gently.

'Conflicted,' Evelyn admitted. 'I seem to get angrier with Seb every time I think about it. I can't believe he's got us into this mess, or that he's lied to me for so long. But it still doesn't seem real, somehow. I know it's a cliché, but I'm still expecting to wake up and find out that it was a nasty dream. It's *Seb* we're talking about, for Christ's sake—my husband. The fact that he's had this hidden life all this time is a lot to process.'

'I think that's pretty normal, angel,' said Jess, reaching over to squeeze Evelyn's hand. 'I mean, you're essentially going through a grieving process of sorts. No, he's not dead, but the man you thought you knew doesn't exist, and your marriage could well be over too. It's almost harder for you than if he'd died... That sounds fucking awful to say, but at least if he was dead you'd have all these sacred, untarnished memories—now I bet you're raking through your whole relationship and wondering if any of it was actually as good as you thought, or if it was all a pack of lies—am I right?'

'You're a wise woman,' admitted Evelyn. 'That's pretty much spot-on; it's what I've been torturing myself with. I was going through my phone earlier, looking at lots of old photos and just wondering how on earth I could have missed it. And yet I still don't feel like it's true. If I hadn't heard it from his own mouth, I would never have worked out that he's gay.'

'Well, he's a smart cookie,' mused Jess, tucking into her

berries and granola. 'And he's had a sizeable incentive to keep his true self under wraps. Don't take this the wrong way, Evie, but the guy is obsessed by his image. Yes, he's had an enormous amount of success and I have nothing but respect for him, but I could be forgiven for thinking that how people perceive him is far more important to him than who he is, deep down. I guess we've had confirmation of exactly that, from the choices he's made.'

'What's your view, as someone who's now married to a woman?' asked Evelyn, curiously. 'I mean, when you fell in love with Zoe it just felt like the most natural thing in the world. You were so matter-of-fact about it that we all fell in line really easily. Thank you,' she added to the waiter who had just arrived with her omelette. It looked delicious: golden, silky and wafer-thin, folded over vibrant green slivers of asparagus. She picked up her cutlery and dove in. 'Oh my God, this is sublime.'

'Glad you like it,' said Jess. She paused thoughtfully. 'I think there's a world of difference between my situation and Seb's. First, I'm probably a lot more fluid than him; I suspect most women are. I have a theory that very few women are a hundred percent straight. Most of us enjoy admiring other women. Most of us get girl-crushes.

'Second, I fell in love with a person. I found someone who I genuinely believe I was close to in a previous life. If Zoe'd been a guy, I still would have fallen for her. Our souls were meant to be together. If I hadn't met her, I'd likely have ended up with a guy.

'Reading between the lines on Seb's situation, I suspect he feels differently. This would all be easier to swallow, in some ways, if he was just a complete player who shagged anything that moved. But it sounds like his position is more black-and-white: he's gay, and he's been pretending to be straight for a long time. Sorry,'—this as Evelyn flinched. 'Only you know what went on inside your marriage. And you guys are a formidable team; you're intellectually equal which makes you great sparring partners, you're both driven and ambitious; you're great parents. I can see that he genuinely adores you. So there's lots of wonderful stuff there. *But* his decision to deny his sexuality must have had devastating consequences for his happiness over the years, and now for yours and even Eddie's, depending on what happens. It's a bloody enormous obstacle for you guys to work around, if you want to make a go of it. I can't tell you what to do, my dear. My only advice is this: you've both got to be one hundred percent transparent with each other from now on. That means no more bullshit from him, and no polite acquiescence from you. The only way forward is tough, honest conversations, plenty of compassion, if you can find it in you to give it, and not being afraid to be vulnerable with each other.'

'God.' Evelyn put her head in her hands. 'That's all very sound advice, thanks honey. But there's so much to figure out.'

'Don't forget that you call the shots on these decisions, not the press. If the message you give the *Post* is: 'we love each other and we have many things to work out as a couple; don't hold your breath', that's a valid response, and it's far more than those bastards deserve.'

'Fair point,' said Evelyn. 'I guess I assumed we needed to have some neat action plan wrapped up for them by Wednesday.'

'No sirree. The worst thing you could do is rush this because of some external deadline. You have ten years and a kid with this guy. Take your time. You both owe that to your relationship, and to your business.'

'Ugh, the business.' Evelyn put her knife and fork together. 'That was delicious. The thing is, we've invested so much in this company. I love it like a child.'

'I know you do. I feel the same about here.' Jess waved her arm around the room. 'They're our babies, our creations.'

'You understand better than anyone; you know what my upbringing was like.' Evelyn's eyes filled up. 'You know how hard I've worked—I worked my arse off to get into Cambridge and then to make it in journalism, but meeting Seb—I mean, that put me on a completely different trajectory. I would never, ever be where I am without him.

'He's the brand, he's the golden boy of the food industry. If it wasn't for him, I may be a deputy editor by now, but I would not be living in Holland Park and meeting royalty. Everything I have now is thanks to him. And does that all go away? If the news hits, and we eventually break up, am I finished at the company too? I refuse to go back and live in mediocrity, Jess, I just cannot let that happen.'

'Woah.' Jess held up her hand. 'Hold your horses there. Do *not* underestimate what you have brought to this partnership. You are insanely bright and driven. Sure, Seb's the product, but any entrepreneur will tell you that a product won't sell itself. You're the one who pushed him to pivot into wellness and look where that's got him—it was an absolute *genius* move. He was the first top male chef with an established customer base who got said customers, especially the blokes, to sit up and listen when he started to educate them around their food choices. That, my girl, was entirely your doing. He'd probably still be offering up lasagne if it wasn't for you. You're an extremely able businesswoman, so don't you forget it.'

Evelyn shifted uncomfortably in her seat. 'That's sweet

of you, but as you say, Seb's the product. If I lose him, I'm out in the cold.'

'No one is losing anyone right now. And there's no way someone as business-savvy as Seb lets his secret weapon walk away, no matter what happens in your marriage. As I said, he's a smart guy. Also, there won't be any mediocrity for you, angel. You guys live a life that the rest of us can only dream of and so the stakes must seem sky-high right now. But do yourself a favour—don't worry about the business or your career just yet. Take it one step at a time. Even if the marriage fell apart, you'd be an obscenely wealthy woman with an amazing brain, who could do anything she wanted.'

'Maybe so, but all those people who jostle for my and Seb's attention would just fade away. I'd probably be a social outcast if I wasn't in Seb's hallowed circle.'

'Who gives a flying fuck? You can't honestly tell me you give a shit about any of those sycophants? You're always telling me how the mums at school pester you guys to endorse their charity events and sit on their boards and come to their fucking soirées—seriously, you can do without them. But let's not catastrophise just yet. Right now, you just need to look after yourself and Eddie, and sit down with Seb and work out your next step. Not the whole road—just the next step. One step at a time, my angel.'

'Thank you, honey.' Evelyn squeezed her hand gratefully. 'I honestly don't know what I'd do without you. I feel terrified and alone right now—it's lovely to have a proper grown-up around to give me advice. But anyway, I'm sick of talking about myself and going round and round in circles in my head. Let's *please* talk about you for a change. How's this place doing? It seems—a little quiet, perhaps?'

'Yep.' Jess looked around grimly. 'It's quiet, all right. It hasn't taken off this spring; I don't really understand why. I mean, it's a fucking bank holiday and we're—half-full? It's pretty worrying.'

'You should be beating them away with sticks,' said Evelyn. 'It's the most incredible place. It's like the Daylesford of Kent, and so close to London. Is it a marketing issue?'

'It probably is,' Jess admitted. 'We have a girl doing two days a week for us: some PR and a bit of social media, but it's not really enough.'

'Are you doing paid ads?'

'A bit on Google and on social, but I'm not convinced that she has an over-arching strategy. It seems hit-and-miss.'

'Yes, you need a coherent plan for paid stuff, otherwise the money goes down the toilet. It's also pretty labour-intensive; you need someone on it the whole time, doing split-testing and tweaking the content and target audience constantly based on what the data is telling you—it's geeky stuff, really.'

'It's way out of my comfort-zone,' said Jess. 'We need to find more budget for it, but the upkeep on the farm and the resort is just so massive that poor old marketing always seems to get to the back of the queue.'

'I can only imagine.' Evelyn shuddered. 'How's your cash situation?'

'Tight. The model really doesn't work at all unless the resort is operating near full capacity.'

'Let me see what I can do.' Evelyn picked up her phone and started typing in some notes. 'I'd love to help a little—if you're happy, I'll have a look through your social channels and see if anything jumps out. I can also put you in touch with some great influencers who'd love a free couple of nights in exchange for coverage. If you've got empty rooms, it's a very easy, low-cost way to get content and spread the word. We could start with some lifestyle bloggers, but also wellness influencers who'd love the foodie side of things. I mean, you grow so much of your own food here, it's just a brilliant story.'

'I love you, Evie, but you have bigger fish to fry right now!' laughed Jess. 'Honestly, it all sounds amazing, and when the dust settles, I'd love some names. But seriously sweets, focus on your own problems for the moment. And when you're out the other side, I will shamelessly pick your brains. It's a magical little place, and I can't help but feel like it's got tons of potential.'

'You're my best friend, and you've just given me some great free relationship counselling,' said Evelyn firmly. 'Send me your social media girl's email. I'll hook you guys up with some influencers while I'm sitting by the pool later. It will be my absolute pleasure.'

7

Evelyn sat in the back of Angus' Land Rover, behind an excited Eddie in the front seat. Angus had even found him a booster-seat. The windows were rolled down, and Evelyn leant back and revelled in the smell of earth permeating the car. Her phone was showing ten unread WhatsApps from Seb. Ugh. She stuffed it in her tote bag. She wasn't ready to speak to him just yet. It was far better to adopt a state of utter denial and enjoy the beautiful countryside around her. What a wonderfully convenient mechanism denial was.

She forced herself to tune into Angus and Eddie's conversation, which right now sounded more like a monologue from Eddie than a two-way street. She'd better rescue poor Angus.

'So, Angus,' she began, 'tell us about the farm. It's changed so much since Jess and my school days.'

'Ahh, you went to school with Jess? I see!' said Angus. 'You must know Bill and June pretty well then?'

'Very well. They were like parents to me. I didn't have a great—well, suffice to say, I spent a good deal of time here during my teenage years. It's always been such a refuge for me. But what Jess and Zoe have done with the place over the last decade is just jaw-dropping.'

'It really is.' The car shuddered over a cattle grid. Evelyn noticed that she had a wonderful view of those powerful forearms on the steering wheel from where she was. 'It's even more jaw-dropping if you consider how deep those changes go. It's not just the creation of the resort, which I've had relatively little to do with, but the complete transformation of the land itself. Bill and June ran it as a traditional, small-scale commercial outfit—maximise the yield of the crops and the livestock, if you like. But Jess and Zoe had such a clear vision of what it could be, and over the last ten years they've slowly and steadily turned the land over to organic farming. The entire place is organic now.'

'I know what organic means,' announced Eddie. 'It means food that's grown without chemicals.'

'Impressive!' Angus reached over and high-fived him. 'That's spot-on, Eddie. In organic farming we can't use chemical herbicides—that's weed-killers—or pesticides to kill pests. We have to be clever about how we protect and feed our crops. We use a lot of poo! And when we rear animals, we don't give them antibiotics and we have to feed them really good stuff. Our cows and sheep are pastured, so they munch on grass and clover all day long instead of grains.'

'My daddy is a chef,' explained Eddie, 'and he won't let us eat anything that's not organic. We go to the farmers' markets on Saturday mornings and pick out our food.'

'That's outstanding!' said Angus. 'What kind of chef is he?'

'A famous one.' Eddie was matter-of-fact. 'He's Seb Macleod.'

'Your daddy is Seb Macleod?' Angus caught Evelyn's eye in the rear-view mirror and she gave an embarrassed nod of affirmation. 'That's seriously cool. I have a couple of his books in my kitchen. It must be very handy having a chef for a father—does he make great breakfasts?'

Eddie considered this. 'They're ok. A bit too healthy. Zoe's are better. She makes us great gophers when she's not working.'

'Gophers? I—' Angus looked confused.

Evelyn laughed. '*Gaufres*. Waffles,' she clarified.

'Ah, I see. Well, you must know a lot about food if you're Seb Macleod's kid. Do you like to cook?'

'Nah. I prefer playing Minecraft.' Eddie fiddled with his door controls and looked out of the window, dismissing the conversation.

'So, the entire place is organic now,' marvelled Evelyn. 'That's such an amazing achievement. What are you working on at the moment?'

'Well, on the maintenance side it's a case of running to stand still. It never, ever stops. The lambs and calves are still only a few weeks old, and we're constantly sowing and harvesting, in both the fields and the walled garden. But from a longer-term perspective, we're pushing even further, making the shift from simply organic to full-on biodynamic. Zoe's been the driving force on this one; she's so passionate about it.'

'I've heard her talking about it,' Evelyn admitted, 'and I know it's a fashionable term to bandy around, but what's the precise difference?'

'Give me a sec,' said Angus, coming to a stop by a breath-taking field of softly swaying, lush green crops. 'Let's jump out here for a bit, and you can have a play in that tractor,

Eddie. I have the keys with me. Does that sound good? Evelyn, wait there.'

He jumped out and ran around the car, opening the door for Eddie and lifting him down. Then he opened Evelyn's door and offered her his hand. She felt a little pathetic accepting, but her ethereal, silk maxi-dress had proven not to be the most practical choice for a farm-tour, and she didn't want to rip the hem—or twist an ankle, for that matter. She accepted his hand and clambered down as elegantly as possible.

'So you were asking about biodynamism,' continued Angus as he unlocked the tractor. He gave Eddie a leg up and they grinned as the little boy started whooping and manically jiggling the large gear-stick. 'It's really the ultimate expression of regenerative farming. Organic farming is a lovely, sustainable way to do things. Preserve the soil, preserve the balance of nature, while you produce food. You're still taking, but you're doing it thoughtfully.

'Biodynamic farming shoots much higher. It aims to transform the land that we're farming and nurture it to its full potential, while simultaneously producing food. It focuses on the wellbeing of the natural world. Think of it this way: if traditional farming is a one-way conversation, then biodynamic farming is a beautiful dialogue.'

'It sounds very inspiring, and compelling, when you put it that way,' breathed Evelyn, drinking in the verdant landscape before sneaking a look at him. His articulate passion was infectious, and very attractive.

'Thank you. I really believe it's the best way to go,' said Angus, putting his hands in his pockets. 'I can get evangelical about this. Mother nature is so much more intelligent than we are. We can't help ourselves; we meddle and we mess everything up with our mono-crops, and industrial farming, our revolting, carcinogenic herbicides, and GMO seeds. Meanwhile, nature knows far better than us what to do. Its ecosystem is so clever, and sophisticated, and beautifully choreographed. Honestly, we're far better off if we take a step back and observe, and *learn* from her about how things work. If we act as a kind of facilitator for the natural order of things, then we can get much better results, and, I truly believe, we can produce more food too, in the long-run.'

'It's fascinating,' mused Evelyn. 'It sounds so restorative, and it gives me some hope that we haven't completely messed up our planet for good.'

'It will be a slow road to get more farmers on board. They're all knackered and disillusioned, and most of them are haemorrhaging financially. I'm pushing Zoe and Jess to let me create some kind of mechanism for sharing our best practices. We learnt everything the hard way, and it took so bloody long. If we can guide other farmers on how to approach transitioning, we'll save them a lot of time and money—and sanity.'

'I think that's a marvellous idea,' she gasped. 'God, this place gets better and better. It's so authentic; it has so many facets. And this feels like a bit of heaven right here.'

She lifted her face to the sun and closed her eyes. She could feel the aliveness of the place all around her, in the sky, in the earth and in the rustling trees. Everything was vital and abundant, and she felt humbled as she stood on the rough earth. London could be eerily sterile despite its charming parks. Here, she could feel the force of what Angus called mother nature. No wonder the Japanese raved about forest-bathing. Being surrounded by nature was like therapy.

'It's heaven to me.' Angus' voice drew her back to the

present. 'Funnily enough, I read theology at uni. That's where I met Zoe—'

Evelyn couldn't contain her surprise. 'You were at Oxford with Zoe? You read theology?'

Angus laughed. 'Is it such a leap of faith to imagine? I probably come across as a simple country oik, is that it?!'

'No, of course not!' Evelyn was flustered. 'I just—I guess I thought Cirencester was the more traditional route for anyone who worked in agriculture.'

'It is. I come from a long line of farmers up in Derbyshire, so it's in my blood. But I took up theology as a bit of an intellectual challenge, really. The irony is that after three years of studying all the major ancient and contemporary religions the world has to offer, I was far less convinced of the presence of any higher power than I am when I just stand right here and let the glory of all *this* wash over me.'

'I know what you mean,' said Evelyn softly. 'It's pure magic. I wish we never had to leave.'

'When do you head back?'

'Tomorrow, after breakfast. It's just a fleeting visit, sadly. We have a big week ahead—I'm dreading it, to be honest.'

'I'm sorry to hear that—about your week, I mean. You must come and visit us again soon.' Angus smiled at her kindly. 'And bring that famous husband of yours. Lord knows, Jess and Zoe need all the support they can get. Right, let's see if Eddie wants to meet some chickens, shall we?'

8

The house felt chilly, despite the glorious day outside. Evelyn sat opposite her husband in their formal drawing room and rubbed her arms to warm herself up. They usually only used this room for entertaining, preferring to congregate in the spacious kitchen and garden room across the hall, but they needed some privacy to talk away from Eddie, who was playing in the garden. The room was gorgeous, with duck-egg blue De Gournay panels on the walls and sumptuous hand-sculpted cornices, but relaxing it was not.

The weekend in Kent had gone far too quickly, and already it felt like a lovely, distant dream. Evelyn had managed a massage in The Barn Spa the previous afternoon, thanks to Mike and Mia's childcare abilities. Then they'd wandered down to the walled garden, where the kids had played in the stunning slate-lined pool while she dozed on a sun lounger. Dinner had been a relaxed barbecue at Jess and Zoe's, with far less wine consumption this time. She'd packed Eddie into the car straight after breakfast this morning and driven home. The dread of heading back to

London, and Seb, had been increasingly weighing on her, and she'd figured she may as well get back and face the music.

Seb had opened the front door as they'd pulled into their driveway. He looked exhausted. He'd picked up Eddie, who'd wrapped his legs around his waist as he hugged his father, and gathered Evelyn up into a group hug. She'd leant into him. Regardless of the tumult of emotions she'd experienced over the weekend, it had been a relief to see him in the flesh, to be honest. It had made her marriage feel more real, and the nightmare that was engulfing them less of a threat, somehow.

Now, she sat gingerly on the edge of the plump sofa and sipped the green tea Seb had brought her. He was watching her cautiously, as if he wasn't sure how to approach her. This could get dull quickly. It was very tedious when Seb adopted his earnest, serious persona. Thankfully, it didn't happen often. Still, she was glad that he seemed to grasp the severity of the situation; his usual cocky self wouldn't be appropriate just now.

'How was Kent?' he asked tentatively.

'It was glorious,' said Evelyn. 'Just what Eddie and I needed. I'm sorry we left you alone—I just couldn't be around you this weekend; I needed some time to process.'

'I completely understand,' said Seb hurriedly. 'I'm glad it felt like a break, despite the circumstances. So, did you get some thinking done?'

Evelyn sat back on the sofa and looked him in the eye. 'I did, but it was more of a shit-show than any kind of linear thought process, to be honest. We've talked about it so little, you and I, I have so many questions, and I don't even know what you want out of all this. It was great to see the girls though. Zoe spoilt us rotten, and Jess had some sound advice, as ever.'

'Oh, did she?' Seb sat forward, eagerly. His body language told Evelyn that he was trying to be open, accommodating. 'What did she have to say?'

'Well, you know Jess, she doesn't sugarcoat things, and she has strong views. She was extremely pissed off with you on my behalf, but she also seemed a little sad that you've felt the need to keep your sexuality a secret all this time—I get the feeling that she empathised with how hard it must have been for you.'

Seb looked at his hands. 'That's sweet of her. I'm not sure I deserve it, but I'm touched.'

'Anyway, her real advice was that this is between you and me, and that we shouldn't feel obliged to rush any decisions just because we have the *Post* interview to get through. She said it's fine to tell them we have a lot of things to work out and no answers for them just yet.'

'That sounds like sensible advice,' said Seb cautiously. 'These people are so damned good at bulldozing you, but in the end, we've promised them a headline rather than a complete game-plan. That exclusive will sell them enough papers; it doesn't matter so much what the interview is like below the fold.'

'We can sit down with Carrie tomorrow, but I suspect that's exactly what she'll propose: say the absolute minimum about what our plans are. Which is lucky, because honestly Seb, I have no idea what you are thinking or how you want to move forward. You've had years to think about this; I've had a couple of days.'

'It's true that I've obsessed about this for a long time,' admitted Seb. 'But the fact that I have to come out to a journalist in three days' time is as hard for me to wrap my head around as it is for you.'

'But what do you want, really? I mean, I'm sure you didn't want to get outed, but it opens up a door for you to really think about what you want from life.'

He seemed to pull himself together. 'I don't want a divorce, at any rate. At least—I don't want this to end. We're so *good* together, Ev. We've built this amazing company together. I don't tell you enough, but I couldn't have done it without you. And obviously we've created a very special family. I'm proud of our little gang; I'd be lost without you two. You know how stressful it can be for me, being in the public eye, being slagged off and judged and harassed left, right and centre. You guys are my home, my safe space. I'm more dependent on you than you'll ever know, and I love you very much.'

Evelyn rolled her eyes. 'While that's nice to hear, Seb, there is this minor matter of your being gay. A marriage isn't just a business partnership. We have that at work. It should be a lot more than that. And you like men! And therefore, you don't desire me in that way. So what are we supposed to do about that little inconvenience? You're asking me to go along with this sham marriage, that you had the audacity to lock me into, without having the decency to be honest with me.'

'It's not a sham. I know how horribly I've deceived and betrayed you. I know that. But aside from the fact that you didn't know about my—other life, things worked well between us, didn't they? Maybe we can keep things going like that. We stay married, we live here together, we work together, we bring up our amazing little man together. And I... see men away from home. And you should feel free to do the same. I know I've fallen short on that front, and I really regret that. I mean, look at you. You're so, so beautiful. You deserve a much better sex life than the one I've given you.'

'Oh, for God's sake,' said Evelyn crossly. 'You're basically suggesting an open marriage. That will never work. Have you forgotten that in five days' time our secret will be splashed across every news outlet in the country? There'll be no sneaking around in Soho after that. The paps will be all over you. And besides, I don't want an open marriage. Ugh. Such a weird thought. I'm either in this marriage or I'm out of it.'

'I'll lie low for a few months,' pleaded Seb. 'The tabloids will get bored and move on. It buys us time to make some decisions together, to try this new version of our relationship out for size. I agree, the optics of my being caught again soon wouldn't be good for our brand. I need to restore the public's faith in my integrity. That's the best option for the company. I'm aware you're still putting a ton of marketing weight behind the *Honest Food* book. What a fucking ironic title given that I'm about to confess to the world that I've deceived everyone for the past decade. I promise I won't rock the boat any more than is humanly possible.'

Evelyn studied her husband's face: gorgeous, blue-eyed, tired despite the tan. Perhaps this was their dirty little secret. Perhaps it wasn't so much the fact that he was gay, but that they were as bad as each other. No matter how much he had betrayed or hurt her, they were both complicit; they were willing to stomach pushing aside their deepest personal desires for the sake of their ultimate treasure: the multi-million-pound juggernaut they'd built. It felt as though they'd created a monster.

'Fine.' She stood up. 'Let's stick this out for the moment. But you're sleeping in the spare room tonight.'

THAT AFTERNOON, Evelyn was numbly checking work emails on the kitchen sofa while Seb and Eddie reclined beside her, watching *Spiderman*. Her phone rang. Caller ID: Lady Adelaide Macleod—Seb's mother.

She slipped out of the room and answered the call.

'Hello, Adelaide.'

'Evelyn, darling. How are you?'

Seb's family was Scottish, but were of the variety of Scots so aristocratic and landed that they spoke the Queen's English. They now lived a few miles away in the illustrious Boltons in South Kensington.

'I'm fine thank you, Adelaide,' Evelyn began cautiously. She had no idea if Seb had spoken to his family to tell them his news and warn them about the upcoming tabloid storm. She soon had her answer.

'I'll cut to the chase. I spoke to Seb this weekend while you and Eddie were away. My dear Evelyn, I'm so sorry that my dratted son has hurt you so much. I just want to wring his neck.'

Her forthright kindness made Evelyn's eyes sting. She wondered how Adelaide herself had taken the news. She couldn't imagine the elder Macleods being the most socially liberal of souls.

'Thank you, Adelaide. That means a lot. I have to say, it's been quite a shock. But Seb and I are both very focused on protecting Eddie as much as possible and keeping things normal for him. I imagine it must have been a tremendous shock for you and Robert too?'

'I'm sorry to say, it was not.' Adelaide's tone was conspiratorial. 'We've known Sebastian was a homosexual for years.'

9

'You knew?' gasped Evelyn. She tried desperately to get her mind around this improbable concept. 'Did he—did he tell you at some point?'

'Good gracious, no,' said Adelaide airily. 'One of the maids found some... publications hidden under his mattress once, when she was changing his bedclothes. She brought them to me straight away. He was living at home with us at the time, while he did his Culinary Arts degree. They were quite dreadful—very explicit. As you can imagine, Robert and I were very shaken. We sat him down and he confessed everything, admitted he'd known he was homosexual for years.'

'And—what did you do then?'

'Did Sebastian ever mention his Uncle Hamish to you?' asked Adelaide in response.

'Your brother, right? Who passed some time ago?'

'That's right. He was my eldest brother, and my favourite. He was homosexual. He admitted this to our father in the sixties and, I'm ashamed to say, my father disinherited him. He lost everything; the estate passed to my middle brother, Cameron.'

'Oh my goodness, that's terrible!' Evelyn was shocked. 'I guess things were very different back then.'

'Quite right, my dear, especially among staunchly religious Scots of a certain class. In any case, he moved to London, and after Robert and I were married and moved down here, we saw a lot of him. He died of AIDS in 1991; Sebastian must have been around sixteen. It hit him hard. He and Hamish got on like a house on fire.'

'I'm so sorry,' said Evelyn. 'How utterly tragic for you all. Seb's never told me the details.'

'At any rate, when we sat Sebastian down and brought up the magazines, he accepted his homosexuality completely, but he told us in no uncertain terms that he had no desire to ever act on it, or 'come out.' He said he had enormous goals for his career, and he had no intention of letting his proclivities derail him. He'd seen what had happened to Hamish, and it wasn't a path that interested him.'

'I can see his point, a little,' Evelyn said slowly, 'but surely he understood that these were different times from Hamish? I mean, being gay wouldn't necessarily have harmed his career opportunities.'

'AIDS was still a big problem at the time—this must have been the mid-nineties, I suppose. So there was still very much a stigma around homosexuality in mainstream society, compared to today. Sebastian always had so much ambition, my dear. He could hold a room even as a young teenager; he knew exactly how powerful those looks were, and he's always been so charismatic. He had a self-awareness I've never seen in his brother or sister. And so there wasn't much arguing with him. We had to respect his wishes, but it broke my heart, you see. Because the thing is, Evelyn dear, that Hamish was very happy. He had a contented, fulfilled, creative life in London; he was a very talented writer. God knows how miserable he would have been running the family estate, married to some girl. Sebastian saw all that, and yet he chose to shut that part of himself away. We would have been supportive, of course, if he'd chosen to live as a homosexual man. It all came from him; that boy has so much drive it scares me sometimes.'

Evelyn considered all this. She'd had no idea Seb had been so close to Hamish, or indeed that he'd had a gay uncle. She wondered if he'd ever confided in Hamish. Regardless, he must have been familiar with Hamish's story. She couldn't imagine what it must have cost Seb to deny his feelings for so long, in favour of chasing a glittering career, as well as significant wealth and social standing. She herself had, mostly, followed her heart. Marrying Seb was the easiest decision she'd ever made. What must it have been like for him? Had walking down the aisle felt like a death-sentence?

As if she'd read Evelyn's mind, Adelaide continued, 'It was all fine until he started to court you seriously. We all brushed the matter under the carpet, and Robert and I assumed Sebastian's... sexual persuasion just wasn't one of his priorities. But, to be honest, my dear, we'd expected him to stay a bachelor.

'Your relationship moved so quickly. When he came to us to ask for his grandmother's ring to give to you, I have to admit we were very taken aback. We've always been very fond of you, Evelyn, and we couldn't in all good faith stand back and watch our son make a terrible decision that would deprive you of the happy marriage you deserved.'

Evelyn looked down at her engagement ring. It was a

huge, flawless diamond that Seb had had Asprey reset for her in a pavé platinum band.

'I assume, given I'm here right now, that Seb won that argument?'

'He did. I'm sorry, dear. As you know, he can be very persuasive. He convinced us he had his emotions under control, and that he loved you very much and intended to marry you. There wasn't much we could do but respect his wishes and hope he was telling us the truth.

'And I have to say, Evelyn, your marriage has brought us so much comfort over the years, especially with the birth of little Edward. You and Sebastian really seem to be a formidable pair, and so we've worried less about him as time has passed. I'm afraid we got complacent. And now this mess… I'm not embarrassed that my son's sexual orientation will be public, but I'm deeply sorry you and Edward will be dragged into this. I'm afraid it will be a torrid time for the three of you. Glen Cova is always available to you if you find you need somewhere more private.'

'Thank you, Adelaide.' Evelyn suddenly felt exhausted. 'Thanks for the colour. It—it helps, to be honest. The last couple of days I've been wondering if I ever really knew my husband at all. This really helps me to get inside his head a little more.'

'You're most welcome, my dear. Good luck this week and be strong. You'll need all that wonderful strength of yours.'

'We need a very, very cohesive plan for Friday across PR, paid ads and social.'

Evelyn was sitting in the chill-out area of Seb Macleod Ltd with Carrie and their Social Media Manager, Gino

Donelli. Given it was a bank holiday Monday, the office was blessedly empty. Tomorrow she and Seb would spend most of the day in preparation with Carrie for Wednesday's interview, but for now Evelyn was keen to plan ahead for the media shit-storm she knew Friday would bring. And the last thing she needed today was Seb sticking his oar in. She'd made it clear to him that he should stay out of it and leave the marketing plan to her and her team. She'd also suggested, perhaps a little too acerbically, that he might want to avail of his last few days of relative freedom from the press by taking Eddie out. He'd jumped at the chance, and the boys had headed off to the driving range.

Carrie, star that she was, had been happy to do the job of briefing key staff members on the upcoming bombshell, on a need-to-know basis. It saved Evelyn the mortification of having to tell people herself and endure their horrified looks and awkward words of condolence. Gino was nevertheless looking extremely ill at ease. Evelyn didn't blame him. He hadn't been at the firm more than a few months, and it was surely a fairly excruciating prospect for any employee to be sitting down with his or her boss to fire-fight her husband's imminent coming-out. Evelyn decided a matter-of-fact approach would be best. She didn't want her team feeling any more uncomfortable than necessary.

'Carrie, can you update us on your thoughts so far?' She took a sip of espresso. She needed the caffeine coursing through her veins to galvanise her through this distasteful task.

'Sure.' Carrie consulted her MacBook. 'One. We have a brief press-release ready to go. It's as short as possible on facts and principally establishes Seb's reasons for coming out—we've positioned it as his feeling the need to live in integrity and truth. You can discuss it with him and see if he's comfortable. It also requests that the press is considerate of your family's privacy at this time. I've emailed it to both of you.

'Two. I've also emailed you a list of our most important press contacts. I will be available to have a chat with each of these on Friday, with carefully selected extra colour on the situation, so they feel the love. Many people will be either confused, pissed off or downright suspicious that we've given this exclusive to such a shoddy outfit as the *Post*. I suggest we frame that decision as wanting to give this story the biggest possible platform, and obviously the tabloids have the widest reach.

'Three. I've compiled a list of TV, radio and press outlets and podcasters who Seb can sit down with in the coming weeks. No one can tell his story better than he can, and the guy is so bloody charming he'll have the interviewers eating out of the palm of his hand. This can be a very, very positive thing if managed correctly. The nation loves a bit of vulnerability. Also, given what a seemingly charmed life you guys lead, I wouldn't be surprised if this makes you both seem more accessible. I suspect this will gain him far more fans than he loses.

'On that note, four. This is good publicity for the book—though I don't doubt there'll be a ton of memes about the word *honest*. In every interview, we get Seb to mention the book and I'll ask each of our partners to mention at the end of their articles that the book is in bookstores now.'

'Good,' said Evelyn crisply. 'That sounds logical. How about *UK AM*? Could he sit down with them ahead of his usual Tuesday morning cookery slot there next week?'

'Definitely. They're already at the top of my list of TV targets.'

'Excellent. Thanks Carrie. Gino, what have you got so far?'

Gino cleared his throat. He looked nervously at his notebook. 'Most important: we need a statement from Seb for social media, ready to post on Instagram, Facebook and Twitter as soon as the *Post* goes live. It needs to be much softer than the press release. I can work through it with Seb tomorrow, and Carrie should okay it too. The image should be a family photo, not professional—ideally something goofy or informal. I think it should include your son if you're comfortable—we need to emphasise what a close-knit family you are.'

'Got it.' Evelyn nodded and made a note on her phone. 'I'll go through some photo options with Seb.'

'Seb will be in Italy with me, Eloise and Laura when the news goes live. We've got some meetings with suppliers throughout the day, but I'll make sure we give Seb plenty of time to reply to any messages of support on social, especially on Twitter.

'I also propose we keep his Instagram Stories feed full of great, product-heavy content from the Italy trip: it suggests it's business as usual over here, and we're putting the health and welfare of our readership at the top of our priority list. We can intersperse the Stories feed with the occasional repost of any particularly supportive comments coming through for Seb on Stories.'

'That sounds good,' nodded Evelyn. 'The footage coming through from your trip will be divine. I'm envious of you being away from the eye of the storm, but I know it's the best thing for Seb. And he's known Laura and Eloise for years, so I know he'll be in capable hands with you guys over there. It will be a strange day for us all. Right, I'd better brief the digital agency on managing our ad spend over the next few days.'

She realised she'd been holding her breath and exhaled. Nothing focused the mind like a good to-do list; it provided a wonderful illusion of control in a situation that felt wildly uncontrollable. She had a skilled team, and they would get through this together. With any luck, they could spin this mess into a positive, where the brand was concerned, at least.

10

Evelyn's engagement ring glinted in the sunlight as she fidgeted on the bar-stool, waiting for the photographer's assistants to clear away the equipment. The *Post* had chosen to shoot her and Seb in their enormous, light-filled kitchen, which was a win. It would remind the paper's readers of what Seb did best, and it was where they both felt at their most relaxed.

The *Post*'s art director had done a decent job, Evelyn had to admit. The kitchen looked beautiful, styled with huge bowls of fruit and vegetables on the marble island-top. A copy of *Honest Food* was propped up behind them, next to the Vitamix. They'd been happy for Evelyn to bring in her own hair and makeup team who had made her look fresh and accessible. It was just as well she'd gone rogue on that front—the *Post*'s preferred look was usually plenty of hairspray, and makeup applied with a trowel.

Seb looked great in a pale pink shirt that showed off his tan, and Evelyn had opted for a denim shirt-dress and her trademark gold jewellery. She'd seen a few of the final selects on the photographer's MacBook and she had to agree that they were as good as they could hope for under the circumstances. The photos of them sitting by the island were engaging, well lit and hopefully made them look like a couple you wanted to root for. Part one accomplished.

They'd spent most of the previous day prepping with Carrie, going over and over the potential questions and rehearsing their agreed replies. By the time they'd finished, they felt as prepared as they could be. The worst part of the day had been the call they'd had to put into their principal investor, Iguana Capital. Edward Chang, the partner in charge of the Seb Macleod Ltd investment, was also a non-executive director and member of their board. He was a tough-talking New Yorker known for his genius at scaling consumer brands and his abrasive manner. Upon hearing the news, his response had been 'For fuck's sake.' His parting shot: 'You'd better handle this very fucking carefully, Seb. There is no room in this model for revenue fall-out. We're watching you. I want an update on sales one week after the article hits. Do not fuck this up.'

The room cleared, Evelyn put on another pot of coffee for all involved. Carrie was whispering with the journalist, no doubt laying down some strict parameters for the interview. The journalist was Elise Campbell, one of the paper's 'least awful' writers in Carrie's words. She was more measured and less vitriolic than many of the *Post*'s journalists, whom Evelyn suspected of having a mandate from the paper to be as bitchy as possible. The *Post* was taking this seriously and had put its best team on it, which was a relief. After all, it was a huge coup for the paper, no matter how unethically they'd secured the interview.

At least Eddie was far away today, at Legoland in Windsor. His school laid on excellent holiday camps for parents who either needed the childcare or couldn't bear the horror of their children having unstructured days outside of term-time. At any rate, his favourite PE teacher, Mr Gilbert, was leading today's excursion, and Eddie had been bouncing off the walls with excitement this morning. Evelyn had walked him down to school for an eight o'clock drop-off before regretfully taking her leave and heading back to face the *Post*.

ELISE CAMPBELL LEANED FORWARD, elbows on the island. The recorder and the back-up recorder were blinking, and the room was quiet, cleared of people except for the Macleods, Elise and Carrie. They'd warmed up by making polite chit-chat about Seb's book. Elise had tried a few of the recipes and professed her undying love for the gluten-free banana pancakes, earning herself one of Seb's famous smiles. But now it was the moment of truth.

'So Seb,' she prompted. 'Why did you invite me here today?'

Evelyn squeezed Seb's hand and smiled encouragingly. This performance needed to be flawless. She wouldn't put it past the *Post* to sneak in some subtext about how tense their body language had been. And she couldn't be sure that Elise was privy to how the interview had come about. As far as the journalist was concerned, she could be giving the interview of her career with no idea that the powers that be at her paper had secured it by holding a proverbial gun to her interviewee's head. Today, Elise was their mouthpiece, their best shot at getting a sympathetic reading of their story. She hoped they were up to the challenge.

Seb squeezed her hand back, took a deep breath, and fixed his blue, dark-lashed eyes on Elise. 'Elise, thank you so much for making the time to come here. I really appreciate it. We're here because I want to be honest with you, and with everybody, about something very important, very fundamental.

'I've been thinking a lot about honesty and authenticity this year. As you know, my latest book is called *Honest Food*. It's been a revelation to write this book, and to immerse myself in the joys of good, honest, *real* produce rather than harming my body with processed food that's laced with hidden toxins. I've come to appreciate how healthy and nurturing it is to have an honest dialogue with the food we eat. And it's got me thinking about how honesty is always the best policy in *all* aspects of life. Lies eat us up; they consume us; I believe they're as damaging to our wellbeing as the worst types of processed food.'

He leaned forward. 'I've been lying to the public, to my family, and to myself, for many years, and it stops now. What I'm about to say next will cause my loved-ones pain, but I believe that we can bear that pain together because it will be born out of truth, and not deceit. The truth is, Elise, that I am a gay man. I always have been.'

Elise was transfixed. Evelyn watched a range of emotions cross her face. She was enthralled by Seb and looked to be on the verge of tears at the empathy he was provoking in her. There was also, however, that intoxicating rush of adrenalin telling her she'd just won the journalistic lottery. This was pure gold.

'Thank you, Seb, for your honesty and your bravery. I can't imagine how difficult this must be for you. Can you tell us more: why have you never felt able to come out before?'

'Well, I made some life choices, and they've brought me nothing but joy. My marriage to Evelyn, and our son Eddie, have been the greatest blessings of my life. I have no regrets.

But decisions like that define your identity and your life. There was no going back after I took the steps of marrying and trying for a child. This has never been about misleading the public, it's been a private conflict within me between my true feelings and the life I wanted.'

'Why did you feel that a straight marriage was the only path for you?'

Seb shifted on his stool. 'Even ten years ago, being gay was far less acceptable in mainstream society than it is now. For me, coming out was never an option. I had an uncle who was openly gay, you see.' Adelaide had given her blessing for Seb to reference Hamish. They'd all agreed that it made his decision to hide his sexuality seem far less suspicious than it may otherwise have. It was imperative to focus this story as a personal struggle rather than a cynical attempt by a celebrity to create an inauthentic image for commercial reasons.

Seb continued, 'I was very close to my uncle, but I saw what his decision to follow his heart had cost him. He was disinherited. He lost everything, and he died of AIDS when I was a teenager, right around the time that I was coming to terms with my sexuality. I couldn't pay that price. And so I chose a different life for myself, and I met an amazing woman who has been the most incredible partner to me.' He put his arm around Evelyn and kissed her forehead.

'I'm so sorry to hear that, Seb.' He definitely had Elise hooked. 'What a tragic story; it must have been so difficult for you. Thank you for being so open with us.' She turned to Evelyn. 'And Evelyn, can I ask how you came to discover the truth about Seb?'

When your bloody paper blackmailed him, thought Evelyn. She fixed on a smile and repeated what they'd practiced over and over again with Carrie the previous day.

'I've known for a little while now. On every other front, Seb and I have always had a very honest relationship. I'd noticed that he was pretty distracted, and we sat down and had a frank conversation. Obviously, it was an extremely difficult and shocking thing for me to hear. But Seb is still my soulmate and the man I fell in love with. He's my partner in life and in work. He's my best friend, and none of those things have changed for me.'

'That's very strong of you, Evelyn.' Elise nodded approvingly. 'And how did you reach the decision together that Seb should come out?'

'The only thing that matters to me is the happiness of my wife and son,' Seb said. 'Once I knew Ev was on board and that she loved me for who I really was, it was like the weight of the world had been lifted from my shoulders. I knew that I could do anything if I had her by my side. And so we started to talk about how it would work if I was to share more of my true self with the public. We have no idea what the response will be like when this article hits, but that doesn't matter. What's important to us is that we're living in our truth.'

'Authenticity is such a buzzword right now for lifestyle and consumer brands,' mused Elise. 'Did that impact your decision?'

'Not in so much that this is an attempt to drum up publicity or curry favour for ourselves and the brand,' replied Seb. 'If anything, it's a tremendous gamble. We know that the fact that I'm gay may disappoint or alienate some of our stakeholders. But we believe it's a risk worth taking. I have a contract with my readers, with everyone who watches me on TV or follows me on social media or has supported me at events. I see this contract as precious, and not to be taken lightly. Hardworking people give me their time and their money, but above all they give me their trust. They trust that I will behave with integrity in all my actions.

'On the surface that means that I will give them the most beneficial advice that I can for their health and wellbeing, that I won't sell them products that aren't of the highest calibre, and that I will help them create joy and happiness in their households through the love of good food. But I can't look any of these people in the eye and ask them to trust in my integrity if I'm not one hundred percent honest about who I am. It's the twenty-first century, for God's sake. It's time we all learnt to embrace each other as the wonderful, flawed humans we really are.'

Elise looked as if she was about to have an orgasm. She pulled herself together. 'One last question,' she said. This was it. 'What happens now?'

Seb looked at Evelyn and nodded encouragingly. 'Nothing,' she said. 'Nothing happens right now. We're happy, we're married, we have a beautiful little boy. We're both committed to taking any future steps very slowly. We have all the time in the world to decide where this path leads us, but for right now, we're staying put.'

SEB MACLEOD TO GINO DONELLI, via WhatsApp, 14:25:

Hey gorgeous. It all went well. Journo lapped it up. 1 more sleep till Napoli. Can't wait for 2 whole nights with you in your homeland. *Paradiso <Aubergine Emoji> <Blowing kiss emoji>* x

GINO DONELLI TO SEB MACLEOD, via WhatsApp, 14:26:

<Aubergine Emoji> Bravo caro. Bring it on xxx

11

'And go! Go! Go! Go! Keep that heart rate high!'

The instructor's voice boomed in Evelyn's ears as she completed as many burpees as possible in the allocated minute. The bass of the online workout's house music reverberated through her body and gave her the adrenalin surge she so desperately needed. It was not yet six o'clock in the morning, and she was halfway through a particularly gruelling HIIT workout.

She'd slept badly but had woken up feeling wired. The article was up on the *Post* homepage and she was sure #sebisgay would be trending on Twitter within a couple of hours. The muted TV screens on the wall of her home gym told her that BBC News and Sky News had already picked up the story. Early morning commuters would be grabbing their copy of the *Post*, with its brutally efficient headline—SEB MACLEOD: I'M GAY—set to send print sales through the roof. Already, every other major news outlet in the country would be jumping on the bandwagon, and God help them when America woke up—they loved Seb over there.

As the HIIT class did an effective job of channelling Evelyn's cortisol rush, she settled into a state of grim acceptance. This was as surreal a moment as those other unforgettable moments in her life: taking a deep breath before she walked down the aisle to Seb and hearing her obstetrician say 'The head is crowning'. Her morning routine felt normal, but everything had changed; this article had set off a chain of events that she was utterly powerless to stop. She'd spoken to her meditation teacher last night.

'Just surrender.' He'd said. 'This too shall pass.'

Both were deceptively simple, if clichéd, pieces of advice. Life would be so much easier if everyone just surrendered to what happened, rather than resisting it. 'Resistance is futile,' he'd reminded her. 'Do not waste your precious energy on resisting what unfolds. Accept it, surrender to it, and use your energy to move forward.'

It was strangely empowering to surrender to the disaster that was unfurling around her. It felt not unlike being strapped into a rollercoaster with no escape. The very act of going along with events felt reckless, exhilarating. At the very least, today should be interesting. Meanwhile, she had a very long, hot shower waiting for her.

THE HARDEST PART had been telling Eddie. They'd sat down with him after his Legoland trip. The little guy had been on cloud nine; they'd all been on the Ninjago ride. They'd eaten lots of treats (which likely meant crap) and got soaked; it had been a roaring success. After his bath, when he was a little calmer, they'd sat in their bed with him and cuddled him.

'Daddy is very brave,' Evelyn had said. 'He's going to tell

the truth about himself, even though it's scary, and we will be so proud of him.'

'I'm always proud of my daddy.' Eddie had snuggled in closer to Seb. 'What is he telling the truth about? Did he do something bad?'

They'd exchanged a glance over his head. 'Not bad, no,' Evelyn had assured him quickly.

'But I should have told the truth a long time ago,' Seb had whispered. When they'd finished explaining that Daddy would be in the newspaper, telling everyone that he was gay, Eddie had shrugged, assimilating the information into his normality in the astounding way that only children can.

'Gay like Miguel and Jackson down the road?'

'Exactly.'

'But they're married to each other. You can't marry a man, Daddy. You're married to Mummy, dummy!'

'Hey.' Seb had nudged him playfully. 'I can still be married to Mummy. We're the three amigos. Nothing can change that.'

Seb had headed off to Naples first thing the following day. This morning, he'd insisted that Roy drive Eddie and Evelyn to school for holiday camp drop-off, and Evelyn recognised that it had been a great call. From behind her bedroom curtains, she could see a couple of paps already loitering outside their gate. Shit. This was real. Thank heaven for their subterranean garage and the Range Rover's blacked-out windows. They'd be able to leave the property without anyone getting a shot of her and Eddie. She wasn't sure if being followed down the street by screaming journalists would be utterly traumatic or hugely enjoyable for an eight-year-old boy. Given his love of James Bond, possibly the latter.

What to wear for a day of being chased by paparazzi? What said 'I'm not a victim'? Chanel, of course. Evelyn selected a mini shift dress in lightweight pastel tweed and her favourite Loewe sandals. Armoured up, she was ready to face the day and get Eddie up for camp.

THE SCHOOL RUN WAS A NIGHTMARE. Paparazzi had staked out the school gates too, so any parent who wasn't already aware of the latest scandal surrounding one of the school's most high-profile parents quickly got up to speed. Evelyn noticed the looks through her enormous sunglasses—the sympathy and sneers that she'd expected. Everybody loved a fall from grace. The British press' greatest skill was building people up and then knocking them off their pedestal in grand style.

The article itself was as palatable as could be hoped for. It was very much Seb's story, Evelyn had noted wryly when she'd read it. The focus was less on them as a couple and much more on Seb's heroism in revealing his truth. Elise had added in plenty of her own asides on the integrity and nobility it took for a celebrity and a family man to take such a step. That was a good thing, Evelyn told herself. It was a tremendous bonus that the paper was spoon-feeding the public with a sympathetic take on their situation. But still, it would have been nice if they'd spared a thought for how shitty all this was for her.

She hugged Eddie goodbye and got out of there as quickly as possible. At least camp today was all taking place behind closed gates at the school's playing fields nearby, so no tabloids could get to Eddie. A day of laser tag and water fights with the teachers lay ahead for him. Evelyn hoped the fun would prove an adequate distraction from what was going on at home.

'Where to, Evelyn?' asked Roy as she sprinted back to the car and slammed the door.

Where should she go? She'd already arranged to stay away from the office this morning. Their COO, Josh, would brief the team, as many of them would have only discovered the news on their social media feeds this morning. Home was out of the question given the growing numbers of paps, journalists and TV crews piling up on her road. The police were on the case trying to disperse them, but still. And besides, they'd probably be holed up there all weekend, held captive in their own home.

'Let's do White City House, please,' she told Roy. That was perfect. The latest in the Soho House Group of private members' clubs, it had a no-photography policy. So no one could chase her in, and no one could snap her. In addition, the rooftop pool felt more like Miami than Shepherd's Bush. Seb, Evelyn and their senior team spent as much time there as they could in the summer, holding brainstorms and strategy sessions poolside rather than in their offices.

'Righto,' said Roy cheerily. He met her eyes in the rearview mirror. 'You doing ok?'

She smiled at him wearily. 'All good, thanks Roy. I'm just going to lie low today.'

She established herself at a quiet, shaded table up on the tenth floor by the pool, ignoring the delicious-looking breakfast buffet and ordering a green tea. Once settled, she proceeded to spend a couple of hours doing exactly what

Carrie had warned her not to do: falling down a social media rabbit-hole.

Gino had uploaded Seb's own Instagram and Facebook posts in advance, as well as a couple of tweets, to be auto-posted at exactly 6am. The posts were a slightly more colloquial take what he'd told the paper—that he couldn't live a lie anymore, that honesty and integrity were a crucial part of his contract with his followers, and that he felt he'd let everybody down. He finished by asking that everybody respect his family's privacy. The accompanying photo was gorgeous—a sun-drenched snap of the three of them beaming, sandy and contented, on Brancaster Beach in north Norfolk.

The Instagram post already had seventy thousand likes from Seb's three million followers. Evelyn scrolled through the comments. There was plenty of trolling ('You fucking puff') and moral outrage from some of Seb's more bigoted customers ('I have been a buyer of your books for five years now and I am disgusted to read that you are a homosexual'), but mostly, the comments were downright supportive. 'This made me cry. Well done you. We are all behind you' said one. Quite a few LGBTQ-rights accounts were jumping in too, with messages of adoration and thanks. 'U've embraced ur truth, our hero' read one comment, followed by many rainbow emojis. Indeed, the entire comments section of the field was littered with rainbows.

Evelyn felt herself starting to breathe a little more easily. Perhaps this would be ok. Some of the messages made her well up. One read, 'I'm a gay teenager. Still haven't told my parents. Maybe now I will. THANK YOU SEB *<hands-in-prayer emoji>*'. She thought of her husband—her handsome, clever, driven husband, and felt a rush of affection. Like everything he touched, it looked like this story might turn to gold. It was almost easy to forget that he'd been backed into a corner to come out; the tale they'd woven seemed so real.

She turned to Twitter. Why was it that people were their most obnoxious on Twitter, or indeed that the most obnoxious people congregated there? The trolls were out in force, with comments that made her head spin. God, she hoped Adelaide had no idea how to access Twitter; these messages would break her heart. However, the supporters were there too. This story was becoming much bigger than just Seb. It was an enormous move forward for the LGBTQ community: an apparent alpha-male with a vast audience of relatively traditional, straight men and women had come out as gay. If nothing else, Evelyn thought, perhaps this would help to further cement homosexuality as an accepted part of the establishment. To her surprise, as well as #sebcomesout and #sebisgay, #sebisourhero was trending on Twitter.

Her scrolling was constantly interrupted by incoming calls. Her phone was on mute to accommodate White City House's strict no-calls policy in most of the public areas. There were calls from good friends, distant friends, and plenty of unrecognised and withheld numbers. Journalists. She declined every one of them; she had no desire to speak to anyone.

A couple of hours into her solitary session, Evelyn looked up to find a stunning blonde standing in front of her. Her hair was scraped back, and she was impeccably made up in that overly glossy way that millennials favoured. She looked like an advert for Glossier cosmetics. Evelyn lowered her sunglasses and raised an eyebrow.

'Evelyn Macleod?'

'Yes?' Evelyn asked suspiciously.

'Sadie Thomas. I'm with the *Tribune*.'

'How did you get in here?' Evelyn looked around as if searching for a security breach.

Sadie laughed. 'Relax, I'm a member. I've been working away from the sun lounger over there and I recognised you.'

'Please have the courtesy to leave me alone,' said Evelyn sharply. 'As you can imagine, I'd really like some privacy today.'

'I completely understand.' Sadie held up her hands in surrender. 'I'm not here to badger you. I have one thing to say, and then I'll leave you alone. Seb is practically being canonised by the press. They all know it would be deeply uncool to criticise anyone who's come out. They're all drooling over him. It'll get more and more fawning in the weekend press—wait and see. Meanwhile, I imagine finding out that your heart-throb husband is gay is a fairly shitty experience, but no one seems to be giving you much band-width today. Let me tell your side of the story. I'm a girl's girl, and the *Tribune* is a far classier outfit than the *Post*, as you know.'

'I'm not interested, thank you,' said Evelyn firmly.

'See how you feel next week. There's no rush. Here's my card.' Sadie placed her business card on the table. 'If we don't speak, then good luck with it all, anyway. I can't imagine how it must feel.' She turned and walked away.

12

Seb unscrewed a bottle of well-chilled Marlborough Sauvignon Blanc with relish and sloshed two generous helpings into a couple of long-stemmed glasses. He handed one to Evelyn and sat down heavily on his sun lounger.

'Cheers, Ev. Well survived. I'm so sorry I had to leave you and Eddie to face the vultures on your own.'

It was early evening on Sunday; Seb had just returned from Italy and they were hiding out in their garden. He took a large gulp of wine.

'Christ, this brings back memories of our New Zealand trip. Do you recall staying on that tiny little vineyard in Blenheim? The owners told the Hans Hertzog winery that we were on our honeymoon and they gave us the best table that evening—remember, it looked out onto their heavenly gardens?'

'I wish I was bloody well there right now, without a care in the world,' said Evelyn grimly, taking a healthy glug.

In front of them lay an incredible spread from Nobu. The head chef had called Seb to ask if he could send it over, along with a bottle of Krug, as a show of support and appreciation from the Nobu team. The house was, in fact, filled with champagne and flowers from fellow chefs, celebrities and Seb and Evelyn's wider network.

'Well, there are worse places to have to hide out,' said Seb, grabbing some jalapeño yellowtail tuna with his chopsticks and gazing around the garden. 'How have you and Eddie found the last forty-eight hours?'

'Friday was brutal.' Evelyn popped a chilli and garlic edamame pod between her teeth. 'There were paps and TV crews everywhere—at the house, at school, and apparently outside the office too. I hid out at White City House most of the day until Eddie'd finished camp.' She carefully omitted any mention of her brush with the *Tribune* journalist, Sadie.

'Since then we've had a pretty quiet weekend. We did a duvet day yesterday which I think he needed actually, after a week of camp. We watched *Despicable Me 3*, ate popcorn and snuggled together in the den. Then I let him loose on the Xbox and basically proceeded to stalk social media for a few hours.'

'What's Carrie's view on how it's all gone down?'

'She seems thrilled with the reaction on social, and in the press. I mean, it all looks overwhelmingly positive. The *Guardian* did a lovely piece on how a national treasure—you—has just become even more treasured. Did she send it to you?'

'She did. It was lovely. I have to say, the feedback's just been amazing to read, and it's made the entire process much easier for me. I'll admit I was anxious about a backlash, but if anything our 'approval ratings', if you can call them that, seem to be skyrocketing. The support from the US has been incredible too; *Good Morning America* wants me on via video conference next week.'

'That's insane!' exclaimed Evelyn. 'You'll have a seriously busy week next week.' She refilled their glasses. This Sauvignon was going down quickly.

'How are you doing?' Seb looked at her intently.

'I'm ok.' She returned his gaze steadily. 'I haven't had a huge amount of time to navel-gaze, to be honest. I've been more worried about you and about how the fall-out would affect the company. The last week's been a complete whirlwind, and not in a good way. But last night I took a bath after I'd got Eddie down, and it started to sink in. My husband is gay, and now the world knows it.' She gave him a tight smile. 'They're both quite large bombshells to absorb. I feel like we've got over the first hurdle, but it will be a long road ahead and a lot of work, Seb, to see whether we can make this work.'

'I know how hard this is for you, and I'm just in awe of the way you're handling it.' Seb's eyes were moist. 'I'll make it up to you, Ev, I promise. I can't tell you how grateful I am. We're in this together. We'll do the work together.'

'Speaking of work, tell me about the Amalfi trip. Was it worthwhile?' asked Evelyn, as she picked at a flake of miso black cod. It melted in her mouth. It was delightful to enjoy Nobu in the comfort of her own garden, without having to endure the City wankers who usually frequented it.

'Oh, God, yes.' Seb looked relieved at the change of subject. 'It was fascinating. And great fun. Just being down there gave me such a boost. We stayed in Positano last night and I treated the team to a few drinks at La Sirenuse. It was spectacular watching the sun set over the Med with a large G&T. I wish you'd been with us. I brought you back some of those Murano tumblers from the hotel boutique; the ones with the coloured swirls. I thought they'd look nice in the glass-fronted kitchen cupboards.'

'Thanks, darling.' Evelyn was touched by the familiar gesture. He'd always been great at bringing beautiful spoils back from his travels. 'Did you uncover some good suppliers?'

'A couple of real gems.' Seb leaned forward. 'Ev, offering our audience access to this kind of food is *exactly* what *Honest Food* is all about. It's not about denial or misery, it's about tossing away all that processed crap that the big food companies churn out and just revelling in the most delicious, organic ingredients, serving them up as they are rather than meddling too much.

'And the caprese salads were to die for. We took some great footage of the seafood too—fishermen bringing in the haul, then locals cooking it up on outdoor grills with the freshest herbs and salsas. It really got me fired up. It's hard not to beat Mediterranean cooking for just the sheer simplicity of it—letting the flavours sing. We've got so much extra content now, to compliment the cookbook.'

'Brilliant,' said Evelyn. 'We need to stay focused, and make sure the company doesn't suffer while we deal with all this crap. I'll sit down with Gino during the week about a strategy for getting all this content properly rolled out on social.'

~

THE NEXT MORNING, Evelyn braved the office after school-run. Seb would be in and out during the day, between media appearances. He'd already been on national breakfast television that morning, appearing to charm the pants off both the male and female anchors.

Evelyn was immensely grateful to Carrie, who'd been stemming the tide of the media deluge. She must feel like the little Dutch boy from folklore who'd put his finger in the dike. But Carrie could handle it—she was a pitbull.

The atmosphere in the office seemed to be one of cautious optimism. She got many awkward smiles from employees who clearly had no idea of the etiquette around this type of situation. She could sympathise—she had no idea of the etiquette either. But the weekend press had been almost unequivocally supportive of Seb, except for—surprise, surprise—a couple of bitchy columns in the *Daily Mail*. There was a real international outpouring of goodwill and positivity, and it seemed the entire office was riding it.

Thank God she had a company to run, thought Evelyn. The effort of managing the marketing side of what was essentially a crisis was all-consuming. It conveniently made it all but impossible for her to obsess about how she was feeling deep-down. The marketing strategy was a delicate dance between fire-fighting and opportunism, between defence and offence. They couldn't be crass, but the size of the opportunity was growing clearer with each day of the press cycle. They couldn't be seen to be pushing product, and yet their Amazon book sales were up twenty-five percent week-on-week and the paid social media and PPC ads they'd quietly put on were earning a brilliant return. Their direct e-commerce sales were up a similar amount. Evelyn allowed herself a moment to enjoy the thought of their investor, Ed Chang, metaphorically sticking those figures up his arse next Friday. 'Don't fuck this up', indeed. She WhatsApped Seb: 'Well done this morning. Sales +25% and press cycle still going strong <*thumbs-up emoji*>.'

A moment later, Carrie knocked on her door. Evelyn waved her in. She was clutching her laptop.

'Have you got a sec?' Her voice was uncharacteristically high.

'Of course. Sit down. What's wrong?'

'Can I kill the windows?' Carrie hit the opacity switch and came to sit opposite Evelyn.

'Evelyn, I have something I need to show you.' She opened up her laptop and then met Evelyn's eyes. 'It's not good. I wasn't sure what to do with this, whether to go to you or Seb with it first. But I figured you've been blindsided enough recently.'

'What on earth is it?' A now-familiar wave of nausea hit her.

'It's the *Post* pap shots. Remember part of the deal was that they'd hand them over? I didn't think much of it until they emailed them through just now. Take a look.'

Here they were, the shots that had forced her husband's hand and changed the course of her life. And once she'd seen them, she couldn't un-see them. Seb, in the arms of another man, would be imprinted on her consciousness forever.

She swallowed, and clicked on the attachments, opening the JPEGs one by one.

Click. Seb leaning in towards another guy, his hands framing the man's face. Seb's face was clearly recognisable. It looked as though he was leaning in for a kiss.

Click. A full-on, passionate kiss.

Click. Hugging. Seb's face could be seen again, over the other guy's shoulder.

Click. The other guy turning to leave. Both faces visible, both smiling at each other. The guy was handsome, clean-cut, eyes shining as he gazed at Seb. He ran his hand through his floppy, black hair. It was Gino.

13

She shot out of her chair and looked at Carrie.

'Are you kidding me? Are you *kidding* me right now?'

'I'm so sorry, Evelyn. I didn't know until just now, either.'

Evelyn paced around the room, biting down on her knuckles. Her mind was racing. What had Seb said, when she asked him about the guy in the pictures? Nothing, really. She didn't think she'd actually asked him. She remembered him saying he'd been sleeping with 'different guys'—he'd let her assume there was no one special. Well, that gaze looked pretty special to her.

'So Seb doesn't know yet?'

'No,' confirmed Carrie. 'Although he may already suspect that the photos are of him and Gino. It depends on how many guys he's been with recently, I guess. What do you want to do?'

Evelyn leant heavily on her desk and hung her head. 'First, I need to speak to my husband. Then I'd like security to march Gino out of this building.'

'Careful. With all due respect, Evelyn, Seb's the CEO.

That either means that Gino is very well protected, or even that there's some kind of Me Too element here. I mean, it's a huge abuse of power on Seb's part. It's fucking stupid, if you ask me.'

'Oh God,' Evelyn groaned. 'You're right. Well, Seb is arrogant enough to believe he can get away with whatever he likes. And to think I smiled sweetly and played the supportive wife for that bloody interview! I'm absolutely fuming.' She looked up. 'Do me a favour. Have a think about solo interview opportunities for me. Maybe it's time I tell my side of the story.'

'That's certainly something we can look into,' said Carrie carefully, 'but I'd strongly advise a cooling-off period first, Evelyn. You've been through a lot this week. You don't want to say something publicly in the heat of the moment that you regret. And you don't want to contradict what you said in the *Post*—that just lessens your credibility. Wait until you've spoken to Seb, at least.'

'Sound advice,' Evelyn said. 'Thanks Carrie.' Once she was alone, she rummaged in her wallet. Bollocks to that. If Carrie thought she was going to sit back and take this, she was very much mistaken. This felt like a good time to give that *Tribune* journalist a call. Now, where was her card?

'Jess?'

'Hey angel! How are you holding up?'

At the sound of Jess' voice, Evelyn broke down, gasping for breath, snot pouring from her nose. She was crying like Eddie did when he hit a wall. It was primal, ugly crying; hot, angry tears ran down her face and she scrambled in her desk drawer for a tissue.

'Good God Evie, what's wrong?'

'It's Seb,' gulped Evelyn. 'Um, we got the pap shots from the *Post* and it turns out he's been shagging a member of my team here, a guy called Gino who does our social media. They were caught on camera together on a night out in Soho.'

'That shithead! He is such a fucking arrogant tosser. I'm so sorry, my dear.'

Evelyn blew her nose noisily. 'It's the arrogance that's breathtaking, actually. He gets rumbled by a tabloid and spins me a tale where he's the victim so that I sit by his side sweetly for the press—now he has the entire country applauding him for his bravery and integrity while he shags a colleague behind my back! Infidelity is infidelity. He seems to think the gay thing gives him a pass to behave how he likes within our marriage and manage me on a need-to-know basis.'

'Have you confronted Seb yet?'

'No. I'll go speak to him in a minute. I wanted to hear your voice first.'

'Bless you. Can you give this other guy the boot?'

'Gino? I'd love nothing more, but can you imagine how it would look in front of an employment tribunal: 'My CEO slept with me and then fired me'—it would be a bloody HR nightmare. And, to make things even worse, they've just been in Italy together! That's the worst bit—while I was here, holding down the fort and trying to protect Eddie from the press frenzy, Seb and Gino were shacked up in Positano, watching the sunset and probably posting on Instagram from their bed!'

Jess whistled. 'That really takes the cake. Angel, this guy is a total sociopath. He swore blind to you that he was committed to the marriage, and he's been fucking someone on your fucking team! I have no words.'

'Which is why I've done something,' said Evelyn tentatively.

There was a pause. 'What have you done, Evie?'

'I've contacted a journalist. She gave me her card on Friday and offered to tell my side of the story; in her view the press is canonising Seb and ignoring me. I'm meeting her for a drink later.'

'Evie. You'll do no such thing. Do you hear me?'

'But she's with the *Tribune*,' pleaded Evelyn. 'She's not some tabloid hack. I looked her up online; I liked her articles. She did a brilliant sit-down with Victoria Beckham recently. She can give me a voice.'

'You don't need a voice just now. The best thing you can do, in all honesty, is take a leaf out of the royals' book: never complain; never explain. You're furious and hurt. And so you should be. But speaking to a journalist when you're in this emotional state is very dangerous.'

'I thought you'd be on my side.' Evelyn noticed that her voice sounded petulant. 'I thought you'd want me to hang Seb out to dry.'

'I am on your side. The guy's behaving like a total dick! But listen to me, my angel. The media is on his side right now. We've all got a great new gay role-model in our midst, and that makes life for people like me a lot easier. You really risk looking churlish, my dear, if you criticise him. Keep his grubby little boyfriend a secret for now. I imagine that's what your PR team would say if you ask them too.'

'I haven't told them,' Evelyn admitted.

'You see? Also, my slightly cynical advice would be to keep a united front for now, for the sake of the business. You have an amazing company there, Evie, and you own a good chunk of it. Couples slagging each other off in the press is not the classiest thing in the world, and you, my dear, are a classy woman.

'Just let things run their course for a few days. I'm not saying you can't sit down with this woman, but wouldn't it make sense to cool off first and get your PR guys involved too? You owe it to yourself to get the best possible coverage. I'd hold off for the cover of Vogue if I were you.'

'If only,' grimaced Evelyn. 'But Jess… I feel completely trapped here.' She looked around her minimalist office, the windows still whited-out. 'There's a media circus wherever I go. I can't bear to bump into Gino—that's Seb's… guy—and yet we need him from a work perspective now more than ever. And it's so *humiliating*, Jess! I'm sure word will get out around the office and I'll be a total laughing-stock. It's just—unbearable. I need to get out of here.'

'Come back down here,' said Jess. 'Pull Eddie out of school, pack a bag and just come down for a few days, or weeks, whatever it takes. The resort is dead this week. The cottage you had is vacant, if you want it. Honestly, Evie, I don't see any upside to you hanging around there for the moment. Just get out of there.'

'But school—work…' the logistics of it made Evelyn feel tired. She didn't have the bandwidth for this kind of planning right now, although nothing sounded nicer than running for the hills and ending up at Sorrel Farm.

Jess must have picked up on her despair, for her tone softened. 'You must be so overwhelmed, angel. Here's what you do. Find Seb. Tell him he can choose between you telling all to the *Tribune* or disappearing for a week or two. Call the school and tell them you'll be pulling Eddie out for a short while. They must be used to accommodating that kind of stuff with all the oligarchs at that place?'

Jess was right. That was one benefit of the eye-watering fees; the school existed as a kind of educational concierge for the parents and kids. Come to think of it, a boy in Eddie's class was currently spending a term in Monaco and they'd held his place for him—most likely while his parents counted off a few weeks abroad to ensure their non-dom status.

'Then, I'm going to come up and get you. I'll get the train up from Borough Green and I can help you guys get packed up and hitch a ride back.'

'Oh God no, that's not necessary, Jess!' exclaimed Evelyn.

'Yes, it is.' Jess' voice was firm. 'Let me help. You've been on your own the past few days while Seb gallivants around the Med with his fuck-buddy. It's time you had a little moral support. It'll be fun. We can listen to nineties dance hits in the car and take a trip down memory lane. Ooh, and we can raid Seb's wine cellar! Bring a few nice first-growths down for some boozy dinners at ours.

'Now's not the time to try to do it all alone, angel. Let your friends help you through this. Now, why don't you sit down and work out what you need to delegate at work to make this happen? And cancel that bloody journalist.'

~

EVELYN HUNG up and marched next door to Seb's office. He looked up as she walked in, and she saw him flinch as she slammed his door. Good.

'What is it, Ev? You look upset.'

'Very perceptive, Seb. Why don't you take a look at these and tell me why you think I'm upset?' She opened up her

MacBook and thrust it at him. The photo of him and Gino smiling at each other filled the screen.

Seb looked at it and buried his head in his hands. 'Fuck. Evelyn, I'm so sorry.'

Evelyn's eyes smarted. '*Gino*, Seb? Really? You told me there were different men. You didn't tell me you were screwing a member of *my* team. Have you any idea how devastating this is for me? How humiliating?'

Seb appeared to be choosing his words. 'There have been different guys, always. That's the easiest way for me—keep that life separate; keep it to just sex. Mixing up the guys makes things simpler. But I bumped into Gino about six weeks ago in a bar. Obviously my first thought was that he would blow my cover until it occurred to me that he was there for the same reason that I was. I hadn't even been sure he was gay, but I'd definitely clocked him at work.'

That part made sense. Gino was absolutely gorgeous. He reminded Evelyn of those guys in the eighties' Levi's 501s adverts, the floppy-haired dreamboats whom Evelyn blamed squarely for establishing her taste in men, and look where that had got her. To a floppy-haired, gay husband. There had been much interest in Gino from the girls in the office, and Evelyn had heard some speculation as to which way he leant. He must be at least ten years younger than Seb, though. She needed to stay calm. She had questions.

'Did you get together that night?'

'No, a few days later.'

'Why didn't you tell me about Gino with everything else?'

'I thought about it, but I didn't think it was a good idea. It's a very new relationship, and I didn't want to put that kind of pressure on it, or put Gino in the spotlight. Also—forgive me, but I figured I was detonating enough bombshells. I wasn't sure it was what you needed to hear just then.'

'You've spent the last ten years deciding what I did and didn't need to know, haven't you?'

Seb blinked. '*Touché*. But I really was just trying not to overwhelm you.'

'Bollocks. You were keeping your options open, and you were keeping me exactly where you wanted me. This time last week I gave you an out, and you didn't take it. You sat across from me and told me that you wanted this marriage to work—you basically asked me to knowingly keep sacrificing everything that I'd unknowingly sacrificed for the past decade. When really, I was Plan B, and you were quietly working away on Plan A, your relationship with *Gino*, for God's sake, while your clueless little wife simmered nicely on the back burner.'

'It wasn't like that; I swear, darling! I was just—confused, and I was desperate to preserve the thing that's most precious to me, my family.'

'Is it serious?'

'Yes,' Seb sighed. 'I know you're just getting your head around the idea that I'm gay, and I know this is far from ideal. The last thing you deserve right now is to be confronted with the reality of another person in my life, but I'm completely smitten, Ev. I can't help but think the timing of this is precipitous, somehow. God knows how I would have come clean about this without the *Post* forcing my hand.'

'Were you together in Italy?'

'We were. And I know how that must sound... but it was very comforting having him there with me in Italy when the story hit.'

Evelyn was seething. It had been such a tough weekend

for her, alone with Eddie, cowering indoors while the press bayed for blood outside their windows. 'Oh, I'm sure he was very comforting. I have one more question, Seb. Where does that leave us? And please do me the decency of being honest for once in your life.'

He looked down at his hands and exhaled.

'Right.' She was determined to keep control of this conversation. 'You have two choices, Seb. I can honour my appointment for drinks with the *Tribune* tonight. And believe me, I'll tell them everything. They're very keen to share my side of the story. Or, I can take Eddie out of school and get out of here for a week or two. Jess says we can stay at the farm. If I do that, I'll work remotely, but you have to leave me the hell alone. And keep Gino well away from me. Carrie manages him while I'm away. I don't want to hear from him. Now, given that you've been the puppet master of my life for the last ten years, I think I'll decide this one for you. I'm getting out of here. Make it work.'

'Mrs Macleod. May I have a quick word?'

Evelyn was trying to creep through Eddie's school's entrance hall, unnoticed by the other parents, when she felt a hand on her arm. It was Mr Whitlow, the headmaster.

'Of course.' She followed him through to his office and he shut the door.

'First, may I offer my condolences. I know that this hasn't been the easiest week for your family.'

'Thank you.' She inclined her head. 'And I'm sorry about —all the media attention outside.'

'Please don't worry about that.' Mr Whitlow gave her a kind smile. He was a burly man with a forthright manner.

Evelyn had always been slightly afraid of him, and she suspected that his don't-bullshit-me style came in very helpful when dealing with wealthy, entitled parents who were used to getting their own way. 'We're quite used to that kind of thing, given the parent demographic here. I'm afraid there was an incident this morning, though. Eddie was the target of some unpleasantness in the playground.'

'What happened?' Evelyn's heart was in her mouth. If they'd laid a finger on him...

'It was purely verbal, but unacceptable. It seems a group of the older boys confronted him with Mr Macleod's sexuality in a very insulting way; they accused Eddie's father of being a 'puff'. I can only apologise and assure you that this is a very inclusive school where any slurs of that kind are dealt with immediately.'

'Was Eddie ok? He probably had no idea what they were talking about.' Those little shits. She would love to give them all a good slap. It was shocking, the violence of the reaction that bullies could arouse in her. Why were children so goddamn mean to each other?

'He didn't seem familiar with the term, no, but he knew that his father was being insulted, which made him quite upset. Though he ran along quite happily after a couple of stickers and a bag of Haribo in my office.'

'Thank you.' Evelyn smiled at him gratefully.

'In these situations, it often stems from the parents. The children either absorb unpleasant terms or sentiments from their parents, or the children can be insecure in themselves thanks to their home environment. I can assure you that the parents of these children have been called in for a chat.'

She wouldn't like to be in their shoes. Seeing her opportunity, she leant forward.

'There's been a development today which has made my

current situation less tolerable. I'm very keen to get out of London and away from this media circus for a few days. If I took Eddie down to stay with friends in Kent for a couple of weeks, would you object?'

'No, on the contrary, it's probably the best thing for you both right now,' said Mr Whitlow. 'All we'd ask is that you keep him up to speed on his studies to the extent that you can. I can organise a few hours per week of Skype tutoring in English and Maths from the floating staff members. And Eddie's form teacher can liaise with you directly, sending you worksheets and reading. How does that sound?'

'It sounds wonderful,' said Evelyn in relief. 'In that case, I'll grab Eddie and we'll get out of town tonight.'

'Look after yourselves.' Mr Whitlow shuffled some papers on his desk. 'And don't stress too much about the schoolwork. Eddie's eight. A few days away from the routine won't kill him. The key thing in these situations is to safeguard his mental health, so make sure he gets plenty of fresh air and climbs a few trees. We'll be here when you're ready to come back.'

14

Evelyn lay on her back like a starfish, enjoying the sensation of the cool water lapping against her hair and body while the morning sun warmed her face. Beside her, Eddie was in the same position and they brushed fingers as they ebbed towards and away from each other.

When she'd picked him up from school, he'd been quiet and a little teary, having comprehended the viciousness of the other boys' intentions if not their words. However, Mr Whitlow's Haribo and stickers had gone a long way to consoling him. When Evelyn had asked him if he'd like to pull out of school for a couple of weeks and spend some time down in Kent with her, he'd stared at her, slack-jawed.

'Are you joking with me, Mummy?' he'd asked.

Evelyn had understood his confusion. Usually, she and Seb were incredibly strict around school. Sick days weren't permitted unless he had a fever, and screen-time was never forthcoming until all homework was done.

'I'm not joking, sweetheart.' She had sat in the back of the car with him while Roy drove them home, and she'd leaned over and kissed the top of his head, inhaling his hair. He always came out of school smelling sweaty and stuffy—why were those classrooms so badly ventilated? Twenty warm little boys festering in a too-small classroom in a Notting Hill townhouse was not conducive to a fresh air supply. Surely they needed lots of oxygen to learn, or at least to stay awake during lessons? The poor little things. But underneath that smell was Eddie's very own smell, a scent Evelyn was sure she was chemically addicted to. She craved him like a junkie. Would it change when he hit puberty and stopped washing and started stinking? She sometimes wondered if it was a ruse cleverly devised by nature to wean mothers off their addiction to their children around the same time that said children began to push their parents away.

Eddie had been even more ecstatic to find that Jess was coming to fetch them. Evelyn and Jess had got everything packed up in under an hour and had even swiped a couple of cases from Seb's wine cellar—some Mouton-Rothschild and a very nice case of Chevalier-Montrachet from Domaine Leflaive. That should make a welcome addition to alfresco suppers at Jess and Zoe's. Seb wouldn't care. His generosity had always been one of his best features.

They'd made good headway down to Kent, with Jess acting as Spotify DJ. She and Evelyn had sung along with gusto to classic bands like Ace of Base and Urban Cookie Collective, which conjured up hilarious memories of their school years. The memories mainly involved doing their homework at Jess' house, while munching on endless chocolate digestives and talking about boys.

And now, here they were the next morning. Eddie should have been at school, Evelyn at work, and yet they were floating in a beautiful pool and watching the sunlight glitter on the water. Evelyn swung her body around and started some leisurely breast-stroke. It wouldn't do to exert herself too much after such a large breakfast.

'I have a new life philosophy for you,' Jess had told her over dinner last night, her eyes shining. 'It may not cure the broken heart, but it will sort out everything else.'

'Sounds good!' Evelyn laughed. 'Bring it on—God knows, I need all the help I can get right now.'

'You're such a self-help junkie, you may have already read the book,' said Jess. 'It's called 'Fuck It'—the book, and the philosophy.'

'Fuck it?' Evelyn had never come across such a book, and if she had, the crass title would likely have put her off. It didn't exactly suggest an elevating read.

'Actually,' clarified Jess, 'there are loads of books about fucking it or not giving a fuck. It's a real movement these days.'

'So how does it work?' Evelyn was curious, despite herself.

'It's delightfully easy. Every time you find yourself worrying about something, you just shrug your shoulders and say 'fuck it.' Or even if you're obsessing about something. Like, hmm.' Jess looked around her. They were sitting outside in the garden, watching the sun casting its long shadows on the lawn. The fruit trees' fledgling bounty shone like little jewels.

'Take this deliciously sugary lemon polenta cake here. Maybe you're secretly lusting after it. Or maybe you've trained yourself so well that it's not even on your radar, because it's contraband. Just say 'fuck it' and have a piece. Or maybe your brain's going round and round with the stress of playing hooky from your enormous business. Fuck it. They'll cope without you. As Mum always says, they'd have to manage if you were run over by a bus, wouldn't they?'

Evelyn laughed, but she had to admit that Jess was onto something. For all Evelyn's diligent personal growth study, Jess had a kind of innate wisdom, or *perspective*, that Evelyn seemed totally to lack.

She'd tried out her new 'fuck it' philosophy there and then, opting for a piece of Zoe's incredible cake as well as another glass of wine. She'd continued putting it into practice this morning. HIIT? Fuck it. Nicer to do a bit of stretching and then read a novel nicked from Jess' bookshelf in the front garden while she waited for Eddie to wake up. She'd lounged on the wooden bench, pulling a throw from the sofa and enjoying a cup of builders' tea with—shock horror—cow's milk, even though dairy gave her spots.

Her new tool had become even more effective at breakfast in the Oast House, when she'd finally succumbed to the granola she'd drooled over the previous week, and added a good dollop of Greek yoghurt and extra honey. She'd even allowed herself a piece of sourdough, and yet, the sky had not fallen. She'd had a lovely giggle with Eddie over breakfast, watching him pour maple syrup liberally over his fat pancakes. He'd kept looking up at her, waiting to be reprimanded. He'd probably had his full day's sugar allowance at that single meal, but—fuck it. God knew, the poor kid deserved a bit of a treat.

She was looking forward to the next part of the day most of all. Eddie had a couple of hours of Skyping with his teachers from ten, under the supervision of Jess' au pair, Aurelie. Zoe had, with her characteristic thoughtfulness, invited Evelyn to hang out with her in the main kitchen while they prepped lunch. Evelyn was itching to get a look behind the scenes. She was a decent cook, though living with a chef made one lazy—and insecure—when it came to cooking. She generally let Seb take over at home unless he wanted a break. Nevertheless, working and living with him over the past decade had nurtured in her a deep love of food, and a growing knowledge of nutrition.

Since she and Seb had embarked on their journey to wellness, she'd noticed enormous improvements in her health and wellbeing. Her skin and hair shone, she lost that near-constant brain-fog that she'd always had, and her energy levels were definitely higher and more consistent than ever before. They both rid themselves of their little pot bellies and that stealthy thickening around the waist. Evelyn knew that she looked and felt better now than she did when she was thirty. But while she didn't want to waste all those hard-won results, a few days of indulgence wouldn't hurt her. She was self-aware enough to know that she could use a bit of balance in her life, especially with everything that was going on.

She swam over and splashed Eddie. 'Right, my little fish, let's see who can swim to the other end the fastest. Then we'll go get dried off, ok?'

EDDIE DESPATCHED, Evelyn meandered through the grounds, taking her time. Jess had been right; the resort did feel quiet. There were a few groups of people whom she suspected to be locals: some well-groomed women carefully doing breast-stroke in the pool, necks elongated to keep their hair dry. There were also small clusters of people drinking coffee and speaking earnestly in the Oast House, their laptops open. Evelyn assumed they were local entrepreneurs or freelancers, lucky enough to base themselves at a place like this during the day.

Otherwise, it was quiet: bad for business, but very pleasant for Evelyn. It was amazing how effective it was to put physical distance between her and Seb. It couldn't be much over twenty miles from Holland Park as the crow flew, but it felt like a different world—a far more benign world.

As she walked along, lost in thought, she heard someone greet her tentatively. She looked up. It was that attractive farm manager, Angus. He was wearing his standard-issue Sorrel Farm garb, and the faithful Charlie trotted by his side. It was surprisingly good to see his face.

'Hi Angus,' she said. 'How are you doing?'

'Well remembered, Evelyn.' His face broke into a grin. She smiled too, enjoying his good looks. 'Are you down here with Eddie?'

'Yes,' she confirmed. 'I've—um—pulled him out of school for a few days. We've come down to lie low and get some R&R.'

He looked down at his wellies. 'I was sorry to hear your news—I read about it in the papers.'

Evelyn grimaced. 'You and the rest of the world. But thank you. It's been a tough week.'

'I can't even imagine what you're going through,' Angus said gently. 'If you need anything while you're here… anything at all, I'd be delighted to help. If Eddie needs a bit of cheering up, we can definitely find him some nice, oversized farm machinery to play with. Or he can come and hang out with us and collect some eggs—whatever he fancies, really. Mike and Mia always get stuck in during the holidays, so we're used to putting them to work.'

'Thank you,' she said gratefully. 'I may well take you up on that before the week is out.'

'Please do. And make sure you take care of yourself.' He nodded, as if to underline that it was a serious instruction, and went on his way.

Evelyn could feel her eyes stinging slightly at his kindness. How lovely it was when humanity positively surprised you. Right, she had better find Zoe and put herself to work. Focusing on a bit of cooking would help keep the demons at bay.

15

The first thing she noticed about the Oast House kitchen was its serenity. She could see Zoe and at least four other staff members working away, and yet no one was shouting or clanging pans. Evelyn was used to industrial kitchens, but when Seb ran them, they tended to be, not fraught exactly, but shot through with adrenalin. Seb prided himself on whipping his team up into a frenzy of activity, and Evelyn sometimes thought he sounded more like a Peleton instructor than a chef.

It wasn't the case here, though. A beautiful piece of piano music was playing, and shafts of natural light poured in through the conical roof of the oast, making the hanging copper pans glow. It looked as though Zoe had kept the industrial stainless-steel counter-tops to a minimum; instead Evelyn could see plenty of wooden surfaces. The plating-up table had the lustre of well-polished oak. There were enormous ranges, and also a huge open fire, where Zoe had told her she preferred to cook. To one side stood wooden shelves packed with large glass pickling jars. The jars were crammed full of jewel-like food—huge, golden salted lemons, crimson beetroots and long tapered carrots with pink peppercorns. Presumably, this was the bounty of the walled garden, preserved for winter months.

Zoe herself wandered through the kitchen in her chef's whites, checking in on her team members. Evelyn caught her eye and waved.

'Evie! Come and meet the team.' Zoe gave her a dazzlingly white smile. She looked golden and radiant.

'This is Lena. Lena is responsible for all those beautiful pickles and ferments over there—she's Polish and has shared this wonderful tradition with us. The ferments use up all the scraps from the kitchen garden; it's an amazing way to reduce waste, and Lena's garden ferment is sublime.'

Evelyn smiled at Lena. 'Good morning, Lena. That's a lot of peas!'

'The gardeners picked them from the walled garden this morning and I'm shelling them for lunch. We'll serve them up in a very simple salad with these radishes, and lots of salt and butter.' Lena gestured to a basket of mixed radishes, rosy tinted with brilliant green leaves.

'A couple of us go over to the walled garden each morning and chat to the gardeners,' Zoe explained. 'We look at what's available and we build our lunch and dinner menus around that. We'll always offer the standard things such as pizza or club sandwiches, but the Garden Menu is where our team puts most of its focus.'

Evelyn thought that surely nothing in the world could be as perfect as a wooden board piled high with fresh peas and radishes, cold slabs of butter, and a good smattering of sea-salt. Unless, of course, there was a large hunk of sourdough to assemble it all on, and possibly a tumbler of the palest rosé to wash it down. The force of the image surprised her, especially after her large breakfast.

'I guess I know where I'll be coming for lunch!' she laughed. 'That sounds delicious, Lena. Good luck with those peas.'

'At the same time that we're meeting with the gardeners, we also have some of the team go foraging around the farm and in the local woods each morning,' explained Zoe, leading Evelyn onto the next workstation. 'Meet Ramit. What have we found this morning, Ramit?'

'Morning,' said Ramit cheerfully. 'The wild garlic is still coming, so we'll put it into a pesto for lunch, and I'll be making some fresh pappardelle to go with it. Have a smell of this.'

He held up a bunch of the slim, dark-green leaves to Evelyn, their starry white flowers still intact.

'Wow!' she exclaimed. 'That's some seriously pungent stuff! How wonderful.'

'It's glorious,' Zoe agreed. 'When we serve this pasta dish, we'll garnish it with the flowers. I love to decorate everything with edible flowers. These guys tease me for it—but it's become a bit of a trademark here.'

'We've got more flowers,' said Ramit. 'Elderflowers, here'—he held up a beautiful spray of tiny white flowers—'which we'll bookend the meal with.'

'Bookend?' queried Evelyn.

'Begin and end,' clarified Zoe. 'We're going to make a wonderfully light batter with sparkling water, and we'll do an elderflower fritter for the *amuse-bouche*, and then we're creating a lovely, clear elderflower and mint jelly *pour le dessert*. The radish and peas will form the starter, and the main course is pappardelle with the wild garlic pesto. So it's a vegetarian lunch today, but we have had a wonderful haul of fish from Whitstable in this morning for dinner, and we have beef from the farm too.'

'There's something about knowing that you're eating straight from the garden, eating something that was a living thing just hours ago,' mused Evelyn dreamily. 'It must give you such a sense of… connection.'

'*Exactement, ma chérie.*' Zoe smiled radiantly. 'I call it *la communion*. It's the same in English, I think. It is as if, when you sit down to eat food straight from the earth, from the garden, from the woods, you are communing with nature. For me, it's a sacred dialogue. I sit, and I taste, and it feels like the most beautiful form of meditation. It's like a prayer.'

'You sound just like Angus!' Evelyn laughed. 'The way you both talk about your connection with the earth is so beautiful and poetic.'

'You've met Angus?' Zoe's eyes lit up. 'When did you meet him?'

'Last weekend—Jess roped him into taking Eddie and me on a farm tour and he very sweetly obliged. It was fascinating, talking to him about the land.'

'Angus is the best,' said Zoe. 'A true friend. And I couldn't think of a better partner with whom to nurture this land. He feels the wonder of nature as deeply as I do, and he is performing such alchemy on our soil. The land is in his blood, after all.'

'Yes, he mentioned his family were farmers.'

Zoe raised an eyebrow. 'That is one way of putting it. Landowners, I would say. They have a very large estate in Derbyshire. It's beautiful there—far wilder than here, a savage landscape, but beautiful. They have a lot of game, and Angus is a passionate advocate of the rewilding movement—of turning land back over to the wild. Down here, his focus is more on coaxing our land into true *biodynamie*, where our animals and our plants can grow in wonderful harmony.'

'I'd love to learn more about it while I'm here,' said Evelyn. 'You both speak so passionately about it; it's very inspiring.'

'We'd be happy to teach you. Now come, see these salad leaves we've picked from the garden this morning. I need to wash them.'

'You wash the vegetables yourself?' Evelyn was surprised. 'I thought you'd have a *sous-chef* to do the prep.'

'My feeling is that if you leave the prep to others, you miss such an important piece of the puzzle—you don't connect with the food as much. I learnt this at *Chez Panisse* in Berkeley. Did you know I trained there for a little while?'

'You trained at *Chez Panisse*? That's incredible! How did I not know that?' Evelyn was astounded. She and Seb had had one of the best meals of their lives at the iconic restaurant, during a dreamy Californian road-trip when Eddie was a toddler. She still remembered the delight of their famous fruit bowls.

'Sadly, I was only there three months. I could have stayed a lifetime. But the universe intervened; I came back to France and met Jess.' Zoe smiled at the memory.

'But what was it like, training there? Did you get to work with Alice Waters herself?'

'A little,' Zoe said. 'She's wonderful, and such an inspiration. She was there a lot, in the kitchen, and on the morning farmers' market trips. Her intuition when it comes to food is very special. She taught me how to use my hands to connect with the food. That means not shirking the prep. Come, I'll show you, if you're happy to help me wash these leaves.'

'Of course. If Alice Waters has taught you something, believe me, I want to learn it.'

'Ok. Put this on.' Zoe handed Evelyn an apron. 'That dress looks like silk to me; I don't want you to splash it.

Now. Here we have some beautiful leaves—mizuna, and some mustard greens. The mizuna is this feathery one here.'

Evelyn fingered the leaves softly and watched as Zoe deftly broke up the florets.

'Now, we don't use a salad spinner or anything nasty like that. Too aggressive. We take a bowl, and we wash them by hand.'

Zoe put a huge, glazed terracotta bowl with a flat bottom under the tap and filled it, laying it back on the wooden table. She started to add the leaves, and swirled them around with her hands, massaging them with the gentlest of touches.

'You try.'

'Sure.' Evelyn lowered her hands into the cool water and imitated Zoe's massage technique. The whirling leaves were quite mesmerising. She rubbed them gently with her thumbs and, gathering some in her hands, raised them out of the bowl, enjoying watching the rivulets of water running down. She was fairly sure she had played for hours like this as a child. Zoe was right; it was meditative. She felt centred and calm.

The irony was that Evelyn usually tried to touch food as little as possible when she was preparing it. Seb was always on at her to get her hands dirty, to use them rather than utensils to toss the salad—it coated the leaves with the dressing far more effectively, he said. But it made her feel squeamish. Perhaps it was just a form of laziness; the more she touched the food, the messier she got and the more hand washing was required.

This was different. This did feel like she was communing with nature. She stood back as Zoe gathered up bunches of leaves and laid them on a clean white cotton tea-towel, dispersing them evenly. She rolled the tea-towel up carefully and pressed gently along it.

'This is a much nicer way of drying the leaves than a spinner. Alice taught me this. We can leave them rolled up like this in the fridge till we need them; it keeps them super fresh. You see, we've washed them and swaddled them like sweet little babies. We always have to respect the food, Evelyn.'

Evelyn gazed at Zoe thoughtfully. How delightful it would be to have someone like this as your life-partner. Lucky Jess. Zoe was not only radiantly, improbably beautiful, but her energy was so inviting too. She was like a swan, except that Evelyn suspected that Zoe was just as serene on the inside as her exterior suggested. Her soul felt timeless; she seemed to be someone who was entirely, unflappably comfortable in her own skin, in her place in the world, and in her relationship with nature. That kind of person was a rare treasure in today's frenetic society. Evelyn hoped that some of Zoe's tranquility would rub off on her. Perhaps she should stay here for longer.

Sorrel Farm was doing her the power of good already. Even in the kitchen, *especially* in the kitchen, the contrast with London was marked. While Seb had made celebrating fresh food a key part of his offering, it somehow felt different from the attitudes of the small team here. His approach was flashier, almost. He loved bright, showy food, and their focus on clean eating was, while very fashionable, a little controlling, at times. Sure, they had both worked very hard to ensure that the spotlight was on what people *could* eat rather than what they should exclude, but at the end of the day, it was quite worthy. She could see that. But it was trendy to be worthy these days.

That was the difference, she guessed. There was nothing

trendy about this quiet kitchen with its gleaming copper pans, its old, worn wooden surfaces and its stone fireplace. If Seb Macleod Ltd was food as fashion, Sorrel Farm was timeless. It almost had the air of a monastery kitchen. Evelyn imagined that this was how holy men and women through the centuries would have eaten, coming together to farm the land, tend to their kitchen gardens and forage in the woods, eating seasonally, heartily and most of all, mindfully. This was food that fed the soul, whereas Seb's cooking was more about optimising the body. They were both valid, but Zoe's approach—to the land and to its bounty—was speaking to some quiet place, deep inside her. Evelyn realised with a jolt that it was the first time she'd thought about her husband all morning.

16

'Ed Chang wants to talk to us.'

Shit. It was Friday, almost four full days since Evelyn had fled to Kent with Eddie. Four days of relative peace in which she'd had some room to breathe, to think, to mull over the probable failure of her marriage. It had been less than a fortnight since Seb had dropped his bombshell and assured her that he was committed to their relationship. With Gino in the picture, however, rather than a parade of faceless, nameless men, that was looking less and less likely.

While the past few days had afforded Evelyn some respite and some welcome time with Eddie, she'd also spent much of it seething with anger and resentment. She was angry at Seb for upending what had been a good, strong marriage and working relationship. She was furious with him for his unilateral decision, all those years ago, to deny his true feelings and attempt to forge a heterosexual union.

That was the real betrayal, the fact that she'd been an unknowing pawn in his plan. Although she had to admit that, until now, the plan had worked out pretty well for both of them. She'd been happy, or so she thought—wildly successful at any rate, enjoying the trappings of their luxury lifestyle and their soaring social currency.

A small part of her dared to consider what she would have done if Seb had come clean to her at the outset. He was already very well known when they met, although the creation of his multi-channel company came later, thanks to her involvement. How would she have felt if this handsome, debonair chef had swept her off her feet in his signature style and then confided in her: that he was gay, but that he had huge plans for his life and he wanted to build them with her by his side? Would she have complied? Would she have had too much self-respect to be drawn into a sham marriage with a gay man, or would she have weighed up her options and come to understand that such a partnership had its own attractions?

But then she may not have had Eddie. Seb may or may not have been willing to perform to produce an heir—God knew, he'd wanted a child even more than she did. But when Evelyn tortured herself by imagining any number of parallel past lives in which she had not been kept in the dark about her husband's sexuality, she was confronted by this fact: this sequence of events, however far they may have fallen short of her ideal, had given her her son. In other words, as her meditation teacher frequently reminded her, everything had unfolded exactly as it should.

She needed to find a way to let go of the anger, but it was infuriating. Here she was in limbo, her marriage and her future at the company up in the air, while Seb was blithely moving on with Gino, free to see him as much as he wanted. Evelyn wondered if Gino had spent the night at their house yet. Probably. Seb could smuggle anyone he wanted past the paps in that blacked-out Range Rover.

Evelyn knew that she had ten years of shared experience on her side with Seb, and she also knew that he cared for her deeply. But she wasn't a hot Italian guy, and on that front she couldn't compete. It wasn't as if Seb had been caught shagging a beautiful young woman—on that front, Evelyn could at least have been in with a shot. This was an unequal contest; she was set up for failure. It also furnished Seb's actions with an air of acceptability, nobility even, that Evelyn found infuriating. He wasn't screwing around on his wife with a younger model; he was being true to himself. Ugh.

She remembered reading once that the sexiest thing ever was shared experience, and she'd loved that quote. How *right* that those sleepless nights with a newborn, the shared memories of Eddie's lisp when he was a toddler, the countless mornings they'd spent cuddling him in their bed, as well as the rush of the incredible wins they'd had with the business, should all count towards the feelings she had for Seb. Their relationship had been like a beautiful patchwork quilt, sewn with care, year after year, growing richer and more intricate as they added more shared experiences. It was an investment. It wasn't supposed to come to nothing.

Evelyn was aware that she'd left Seb and the company hanging somewhat when she'd absconded down to Kent. She'd been keeping things ticking over from down here, spending a few hours a day on email, chatting to Carrie daily and batting back balls where she could. But she was uncharacteristically unengaged. And while getting out of there had been the only feasible option for her, it was terrible timing for the company. The media was still all over them, and this was boosting all of their channels: book sales were still up, subscribers to their podcast had jumped, and their Westbourne Grove café, Seb's Kitchen, was doing a roaring trade.

Offers and requests poured in: could Seb speak about diversity and integrity at the upcoming Goldman Sachs Partners' Conference in New York? Several MPs wanted him to take part in a white paper around the next wave of LGBTQ rights in industry. Sir Elton John was keen to book Seb in as chef and co-host for his and David's next charity gala. Celebrities had been busy re-posting old photos of themselves with him, keen to get in on the action, and Seb had gained almost a million new Instagram followers over the previous week. It was all PR gold-dust, and would have been very exciting had Evelyn not been the one paying the price for all of this. It felt beyond surreal to see Seb and their brand flourishing while her marriage crumbled and the life she'd built for herself spiralled out of control.

And now they had to get Ed Chang off their backs.

'What does he want?' she asked Seb. 'He's got nothing to complain about given the sales numbers we're seeing at the moment.'

'He's happy about the sales numbers. He—' Seb cleared his throat. 'He's aware that you're spending some time away from the office, and I felt it best to fill him in on Gino. After all, he's the majority shareholder, and I know my relationship with Gino is risky from an employment law perspective.'

'Oh, that's just great,' said Evelyn. 'The last thing we need right now is Ed breathing down our necks.'

'Well, Iguana does own sixty percent of the company,' Seb pointed out. 'This is one of their biggest investments. You can't expect them to sit back and ignore what's going on. When do you think you can come back? I realise this is a tough time for you, but we need you here.'

'I am grieving right now, Seb, because thanks to you, my marriage is falling apart and I'm probably a laughing-stock at the office. I need you to give me some time—I don't know, a few weeks. Right now there is absolutely no way I can come back and be expected to work with Gino. God! I can't believe you've put me in this position.'

'I really am sorry, Ev. I never, ever meant for things to happen like this. I've made a royal mess of everything. But it feels good not to have to lie to you anymore. How's Eddie? When can I see him?'

'He's great, but he misses you. Just because I don't want to see you, doesn't mean he shouldn't. I'm not willing to set foot in London until all this has blown over, though. Why don't you take him to the seaside for a few nights? Go down to the Witterings—wherever. He'd love it.'

'I'll do that,' said Seb. 'We'll have a ball. Right, are you ready for me to get Chang on the line?'

He dialled Ed in, and soon Evelyn heard his brusque voice.

'What's going on, guys?'

'Sales have been great, Ed,' said Seb. 'All of Ev's team's PR efforts have been amazing. My TV appearances and all the press have really boosted book sales and my paid online courses. Overall, we're tracking about twenty percent ahead of budget for this month.'

'Good. Evelyn—what's up with you? We need you to get back to work.'

'I'm working remotely,' said Evelyn evenly. 'Everything's under control.'

'I beg to differ. We need you in the office, on the front foot. What's the score with this guy you're fucking, Seb? I mean, this is a fucking lawsuit waiting to happen. Get rid of him. Do you hear me? Pay him off and get him to sign an NDA. I don't want to hear about him again.'

'He stays.' Seb's voice was steely. 'No one's signing a non-disclosure. I'm done with lying. I'm not gagging anybody. We can trust him. I promise. I'll make a statement to the board that I'm officially in a relationship with him, so it's all on-record.'

Officially in a relationship. Although she'd known it was coming, it was like a gut-punch. Still, there was no way she was going to react in front of Ed. He'd just accuse her of being 'emotional'. Her best bet was to be steely and professional. 'I'm ok with that,' she said, through gritted teeth. 'He's excellent at his job. We need him in place.'

'Fine,' said Ed. 'But there are no sacred cows here. This is a nine-figure investment for us. I don't have to remind you what's at stake. You've bought yourselves some time with those sales figures. I'll be monitoring the situation carefully. Evelyn—take some time and then get back to your fucking job. Seb, try to keep your dick in your pants and your eye on the prize. I want a full board meeting three weeks from now so we can assess the fall-out and establish what this looks like going forward. Christ, this is the problem with getting into bed with a husband-and-wife team. I'll see you the at the end of the month—Chrissie will reach out on dates.'

17

Evelyn was lying by the walled garden pool with Eddie. Rather, she was lying *under* Eddie. She'd been so enraged by her call with her philanderer of a husband and arsehole of an investor that she'd promptly taken Eddie down here. *Fuck it.* They'd had an enormous lunch on their sun loungers: club sandwiches and apple pie sundaes (how, *how*, had she never encountered the sublime concept of apple pie muddled up in a glass with cream and ice cream before?). She'd also had a cheeky, but much-needed, glass of rosé to help restore her personality. Then she'd started reading some of the latest *Alex Rider* book to Eddie, and together they'd hatched a plan to alternate each chapter with a dip in the pool.

Much to her surprise, Evelyn was enjoying the book immensely. It was kind of like James Bond, but starring a teenage boy, and it was extremely well written. She was reclining on the lounger and Eddie was wrapped up in a coffee-and-white striped Sorrel Farm towel, nestled on top of her. His damp head was resting under her chin and she could kiss the top of it, as far as his temple. She loved kissing the spot on his hairline, where the tiniest, softest, blond baby hairs grew. His hair still lightened up in the summer, but to a slightly lesser extent each year. By the time he hit his teens, he'd surely be as dark-haired as his father.

She inhaled him, wondering why skin always smelt so good after being in the sun. It was a very particular smell, and one that she adored. She'd even been known to sniff her own skin after sunbathing, trying to capture the scent, but the effect was even more pronounced on Eddie. She stroked his bare arm. He was such a skinny little thing, like a lollipop. He'd been a chunky monkey when he was a baby, and a robust little toddler. That had suited her fine. She adored fat babies! But then he'd just stretched and stretched without seeming to gain any girth, like the character Mike TV in *Charlie and the Chocolate Factory*. She could close her thumb and forefinger around his upper arm. It wasn't for lack of eating, though. He put away a staggering amount of pizza when given the chance. He must have hollow legs. Lucky little lad.

Eddie stirred, his bony little elbow digging into her ribs. Ouch. She grimaced silently.

'Mummy, d'you mind if we stop reading? I'm a bit bored.'

'Of course, darling.' She gave him another kiss. It was a shame he didn't want to read anymore; she'd been getting quite into Alex Rider and his impressive stunts.

Eddie shot up. 'Mummy!' He shouted. 'Mummy! There's Jess and Zoe! And Mike and Mia! MIKE! MIA! OVER HERE!' He jumped up and down, waving his arms.

Evelyn cringed. If only he had a volume control, he would be perfect beyond words. *Embrace the child you have*, she told herself sternly. He was pretty near perfect, anyhow.

The others spotted them straight away—strangely

enough—and ambled over. The kids were in swim gear, and Jess held an ice bucket with a bottle of rosé sticking out.

'I thought you might need a top-up,' she said, putting the bucket down on the little table next to the lounger. 'We can make sure you maintain a steady rosé buzz over the course of the afternoon. How are you doing?'

'I'm much better after an afternoon of your delicious food and some Eddie-therapy, thanks.' Evelyn shifted herself up and sat sideways on her lounger. 'Maybe I can bury my head in the sand forever and never show my face in London again?'

'Be my guest.' Jess paused from uncorking the bottle of wine to drop a kiss on the top of Evelyn's head. 'We'd love nothing more. Stay as long as you want. It's nice having a couple of paying guests, for starters! I'm only kidding,' she added, seeing the look on Evelyn's face.

'I know you are, but is it really that bad?' Evelyn felt horrible knowing that Jess and Zoe were so worried about money right now, while she was dripping in cash. She wished she had a way to help them. She couldn't even drum up support by posting content on social media. She only had one hundred thousand Instagram followers to Seb's four-ish million, but it was still a decent following. However, she couldn't risk the press knowing first, where she was right now, or second, that she was not at work—she'd be fighting off journalists before she could say paparazzi. Although... it wasn't an awful idea. Leak her location, get the world's press down here, and instantly this beautiful resort would hit the front pages alongside her. If she didn't have Eddie to consider, she'd probably contemplate throwing herself under the bus for Jess and Zoe. But there had to be a better way.

'It's pretty bad,' Jess said, pouring out three glasses and

handing them around. Eddie was already back in the pool and so she and Zoe took the spare sun lounger and sat sideways, facing Evelyn. 'Bookings haven't picked up for July and August; we're not covering our costs.'

'How's the farm doing? Does it wash its face?'

'Just about,' said Zoe, 'but the problem with the farm is it's too small scale. We need to scale it up to make it worthwhile—that's what Angus and I are working on, but it's a slow process because we are also trying to cultivate a biodynamic way of farming. We can't just spray on the RoundUp and supersize our crops. We could increase our production in some areas pretty easily, especially in the walled garden, but we don't have the distribution to justify it. We supply the restaurant and a couple of local gastropubs; we also have the tiny little farm-shop in the courtyard, but it's quite ad hoc. We sell surplus food; we don't have a strategy for it.'

'It must be so frustrating for you,' said Evelyn, taking a sip of wine. 'The opportunity for the farm is massive, but it sounds like that's a slow-burn. Whereas the resort looks incredible, and you just need those reservations to get the place buzzing.'

'Exactly,' agreed Jess, putting her arm around her wife.

'You need an event,' said Evelyn thoughtfully. 'Running social media ads will only get you so far, and you won't drum up interest quickly enough to fill out those peak-season slots. You need something that will sell the dream and give everyone such major FOMO that they'll be falling over themselves to book this place up. Do you do many events?'

They shrugged. 'Small ones—for locals, or for foodies—lunches, that kind of thing. We haven't done anything major,' Jess said. 'Don't worry, if we had, you would have been invited!'

Evelyn's mind was working faster now; the rosé was firing through her veins. 'When Soho Farmhouse first opened, I remember they hired the place out to a couple of brands exclusively. These brands invited tons of influencers, and suddenly the resort was all over Instagram. There were photos of their green bikes everywhere, and of beautiful people bathing in their outdoor bathtubs. They sold the lifestyle so well. Never do the work yourself if you can get other people do to it for you.'

'So you think we should work with a brand?' asked Zoe.

'Not necessarily. It's great if you can, because you can charge them a fortune. But you should consider throwing a summer party. Daylesford does their summer festival every year, and it's heaven. You'll definitely need some budget. But the most appealing part of the proposition—giving the top guests a free overnight stay—is relatively cheap for you because you have the accommodation sitting there, waiting to be used.'

'How would we get the influencers, or the press, to come on board?' asked Jess. 'Have you had much luck with those emails you sent out?'

'Not really,' admitted Evelyn, 'but people are apathetic. If you throw out an open invitation, they'll often ignore it. But if you give them a hard date and tell them that all their biggest nemeses will be there, then you're appealing to their sense of FOMO which, let's face it, is what drives every influencer.

'I'm happy to put my name behind this. I've taken so many photos of the resort, the planting beds and the kitchen the last few days. I haven't posted any online because I'm here incognito. But I can package these up and send them to the right people when I target them. Everyone's going to the same parties and doing the same thing, day in, day out.

They're all desperate to give their Instagram feeds an edge, to be invited to something that's new and slightly different. It doesn't need to be a massive party. Actually, it's even better if it's a very exclusive invitation.'

She waved her hand at the large stretch of lawn that separated the walled garden's pool area from the raised planting beds.

'Imagine this place at dusk. You put a long, long trestle table across the lawn. It's beautifully decorated with your gorgeous apothecary bottles and local wild flowers and foliage. There are strings of fairy lights adorning this entire garden. All the food is seasonal, from the farm, cooked by you guys. We could have a jazz band in the corner, and pizzas from that oven at midnight. I mean, this garden is a party-planner's dream. It has so much potential. The beauty of a smaller dinner is that the influencers get access to *you*. You're both so inspiring, so authentic and passionate, that they will fall in love with you both! And you let these people tell your story to the world.'

She took a gulp of rosé. She could see the scene so clearly: the softly lit garden, the sound of chatter and glasses clinking, and the heady smell of the rambling roses on the walls and of the abundant herbaceous borders. It would be nothing short of magical. Jess and Zoe were sitting on a gold-mine, she was sure of it. They just needed a little help to unlock it. Forget her money, this was how she would help them.

She looked up and saw that they were both grinning.

'I *love, love, love* it,' pronounced Jess. 'God, you are so fucking clever. Zo, what do you think?'

Zoe's eyes were shining. 'It sounds perfect—very us. Low key, focusing on making connections with people and on feeding them with what we've grown on our land. It sounds very special, Evie. Thank you. Can we pull it off this summer?'

'Let's see.' Evelyn unlocked her phone. 'It's the first week of June already. I would say we should have it before the private schools break up in mid-July—otherwise we've lost people to their vacations. How about the first Friday in July? That gives us a month. And you never know, some guests may make a long weekend of it.'

'You think we can pull off the planning in that time-frame?' Jess looked worried. 'It sounds tight to me.'

'Trust me, with the right people in place, we can,' Evelyn assured her. 'There are professionals who can do this kind of thing in their sleep. Oh girls, are you happy to let me run with this? It's exactly the kind of passion project I need to keep my mind off my personal life!'

'We are, if you can handle it?' asked Jess. 'You have a lot on your plate right now, Evie.'

'I promise you I can. I won't let you down. And now, if you'll excuse me for a sec, I have just the woman to style this party. She's insanely creative, and she's divine. You'll love her. I'll see if she's free.'

18

Evelyn hadn't been able to stop thinking about the upcoming party, or about the potential of the farm itself. She was well aware that both were diversionary tactics, but they were so effective that she didn't care. She reminded herself that she controlled the thoughts that passed through her head. She could fill her brain with images of her husband in Gino's arms, or she could spend her time conjuring up magical movies in her mind, where figures flitted across a candlelit garden, journalists wrote glowing reviews of the resort, and the farm burst forth with all manner of bounty.

Evelyn's inner world was often far richer than her outer one. It had certainly been thus as a teenager, when her imagination had carried her far away from her parents' cramped little post-war house with its pebble-dash exterior. She'd visualised worlds of wealth, grandeur and success, of dashing men (wearing 501s, naturally) and palatial homes, of infinity pools and white beaches. The major revelation had turned out to be her power to manifest all of it.

This vision been the key to her professional success. Seb

had raw talent, grand ambitions, and bucket loads of charm. Evelyn had the ability to see how things could be and to make them so. Her finely honed childhood skill for fabricating realms was, it turned out, a valuable commercial skill. So people wanted a little taste of Malibu in Notting Hill? She gave them Seb's Kitchen, a space so perfectly conceived that it allowed customers to forget, for a few precious moments, their reality beyond its doors. It was she who conjured up glossy, verdant living walls, sleek white resin islands and wicker pendant lamps for their event space. Sure, Seb was the product, but over the years Evelyn created a universe for him that was so beautiful, so immersive, so aspirational, that it became as large a part of their brand as Seb himself.

There was still so much further to take Seb Macleod Ltd. The next obvious step was to develop it as a fully fledged lifestyle brand, with soft furnishings, crockery, glassware, cutlery and, of course, cookware. But for the moment, the potential that she saw in this charming resort distracted her mind's eye. Sorrel Farm was already a beautifully executed experience, and it had so much more to give.

Evelyn's enthusiasm had been contagious. Zoe and Jess were equally excited about the upcoming party, and the three of them buzzed with ideas. Evelyn was intent on the guests receiving an education on how the farm worked as a whole, how important the transition to biodynamic farming would be, and how the farm's produce fed into the resort. The beauty of Sorrel Farm lay in its authenticity.

She'd also been mulling Zoe's comments around scaling up the farm's production by building out some form of distribution. Surely that was something they could achieve relatively quickly, and if they played their cards right, they could piggy-back on the publicity that the party would generate to raise awareness of the farm's produce. There were so many strands there. Evelyn knew that if they were properly woven into a cohesive whole, Jess and Zoe would have a compelling business on their hands. The challenge was how to do it.

To that end, they'd decided to have a strategy dinner. This evening, Angus would join the three of them at the farmhouse for a good brainstorm on how to monetise the farm further. They'd also discuss how to reimagine their marketing campaign to underscore the symbiotic relationship between the farm and the resort.

The dinner would also serve a secondary purpose—to enjoy a few of Seb's bottles of wine alongside Zoe's cooking. She pulled a couple of bottles of the white burgundy out of the cottage's tiny fridge and stuffed them in a large jute bag with three bottles of the claret. She called to Eddie, and they were on their way.

EVELYN COULDN'T REMEMBER the last time she'd laughed so much. Everyone, it seemed, was in a particularly silly mood that night. The free-flowing booze had helped. Angus had brought along a bottle of champagne, which they made quick work of over nuts and crisps, before cracking open both bottles of white.

As the weather seemed intent on continuing its unbroken spell of sunshine, they were eating in the garden while the kids (and probably Charlie the spaniel) gorged on Jess' signature nachos in front of the TV. Jess and Zoe had shunned a sit-down starter in favour of a delicious mezze platter, so they could all mill around while Zoe tended to something on the barbecue that smelt delicious.

'Is that a leg of lamb?' enquired Evelyn, grabbing a juicy olive and peering over Zoe's shoulder.

'Close. It's hogget.' Zoe lowered the lid of the barbecue.

'What the bloody hell,' asked Evelyn, 'is hogget? It sounds like something out of a Tolkien novel.' She took a swig of wine and adjusted the flounce on her top. She'd gone for a low-key look for tonight—low-key for her, at any rate. She had on ankle-skimming jeans and flip-flops with a cotton off-the-shoulder top. The top was a wide custard yellow and white stripe, with a deep flounce.

Evelyn had figured that she might as well show off her fledgling tan. She was usually a sun cream addict, but the last few days lying by the pool had been so idyllic that she'd let herself develop a bit of colour. She'd dressed as if she were on holiday, changing for sundowners after a day by the pool (which was pretty much how she'd spent her day). She'd moisturised her sun-kissed shoulders and arms, kept her makeup low key and dewy aside from a red lip, tied her still-damp hair back in a low chignon, and completed the look with large gold hoop earrings.

She rarely allowed herself much latitude to enjoy her own appearance, but she felt good tonight, and she suspected she looked good too. She'd known that she might be overdressed beside Zoe and Jess, but she'd been conscious that Angus would be there and she had discerned a vague, unarticulated desire to look good for him. She hadn't wanted to think too much about her reasons.

'Hogget, oh child of the city,' said Jess, 'is lamb that's a year or so old. The new lambs won't be ready for slaughter till later in the summer. So the hogget on the barbecue was born last spring and has spent a very happy year stuffing his face on clover and grass and other delicious things. Which is nice for him, and nice for us, because the meat is more fully flavoured than new-season lamb.'

'I never knew that,' marvelled Evelyn. 'I learn something new every day here.'

'They're sweet little things,' said Angus. 'And we're seeing an increase in demand for hogget across the UK; it's becoming more fashionable.'

'This little hogget is ready,' announced Zoe. 'While I rest it, can one of you please help me carry the sides through from the kitchen?'

As she and Angus headed through to the house, Jess drained her glass and flashed Evelyn a look. 'You're looking particularly beautiful tonight. I mean, you're obnoxiously pretty at the worst of times, but you really look gorgeous. The tan suits you.'

'Thank you honey,' said Evelyn, reaching over to refill both their glasses. 'I think this entire place suits me.'

Jess wiggled her eyebrows. 'It's very kind of you to make such an effort for me and Zoe,' she said pointedly.

Evelyn matched her gaze. 'It was no trouble,' she replied evenly. Jess loved to stir, and Evelyn would not give her the satisfaction of rising to it.

'We're not the only ones who seem to appreciate the fruits of your efforts,' Jess added innocently, taking a sip of her wine. 'God, this is fucking good. I wish we could drink this stuff all the time. Here's to Seb.'

'I have no idea what you mean.' Evelyn shot her a warning look.

'Angus seems to be enjoying the view too,' said Jess airily. 'When you were talking to Zoe by the barbecue, I caught him gazing longingly at your delicious, golden shoulder like a starving puppy.'

'Jessica Holmes!' Evelyn could feel herself blushing.

Damn it. She swatted Jess on the arm. 'Shut your mouth. You are talking utter bollocks.'

'Hee hee!' Jess was positively gleeful. 'I'm just saying, if those shoulders of yours get cold later, I'm sure he won't give you the cold shoulder. Know what I mean? Maybe he can do a cinema sneak at the table.' With her free hand, Jess mimed an arm crawling creepily around Evelyn's back towards her far shoulder.

'Will you fuck off?'

'Ooh! I made the saintly Evelyn Macleod swear. I must have hit a nerve.' Jess giggled helplessly, and Evelyn joined in. The problem was that Jess' filthy laugh had always been *way* too infectious. She'd lost track of the amount of times those shared, debilitating fits of giggles had got them into trouble at school.

'You're such a brat. I'm going through a very tough time right now. It wouldn't kill you to be more supportive.' Evelyn tried to look injured.

'I am being supportive! I'm trying to hook you up with the most gorgeous, lovely specimen of manhood I know. Fuck me, after what you've told me about your sex-life over the past ten years, you must need a good seeing-to. If I was straight, I'd definitely do him!'

'Oh my God, please shut up,' Evelyn muttered, her eyes darting to the kitchen door in a panic. 'I'm still married! And I'm not ready for anything like *that*. Anyway, I'm sure he's married too.'

'Well, I'll help you out here, because I'm sure you've never cast any fleeting glances at his ring finger,' said Jess coyly. 'He's not. He's divorced. A couple of years ago now; his ex was a total bitch. And his kids are at uni. *And* he's practically a real-life Mr Darcy. Except that he's the youngest son, so poor little Angus inherited nothing except a nice fat trust fund. But I'm sure you can console each other very thoroughly—oh shit, here they come. Let us speak no more of this forbidden love, my friend.'

Evelyn gave her one last shove as she tried valiantly to straighten her face. Jess was a bloody nightmare.

Angus and Zoe came out of the kitchen, bearing platters of salad and couscous and talking earnestly about the pH balance of the kitchen garden soil, to find Evelyn and Jess immersed in some kind of private joke. They were clinging to each other, bent nearly double with laughter while they clutched their empty wine-glasses.

'Wow, what on earth are you two smoking out here?' asked Angus, setting down the salad. 'And where can I get some?'

This set them both off again.

'Dearest Angus,' said Jess, smiling at him fondly. 'Why don't you come and sit here? And Evie, you can sit here. *Right* next to Angus.' She beamed at them both and Evelyn shook her head warningly.

'Zoe, this looks delicious, thank you,' she said. The lamb was perfectly pink, and the warm rice salad glistened with jewel-like pomegranate seeds. Zoe had covered it with fresh coriander, and the fragrance wafted off the platter as the steam hit the herbs.

'*Merci, ma chérie.*' Zoe blew her a kiss. 'I thought we would take a trip to the Middle East tonight. The hogget has been marinating in harissa for a couple of days. And here we have some blackened aubergine with tahini. Please, please, eat up. *Bon appétit.*'

They charged their red wine glasses, freshly filled by Angus with the decanted Mouton Rothschild, and chorused '*Bon appétit.*'

As a strategy dinner it was a total failure, but it was one of the most entertaining evenings Evelyn could remember. The claret was something else and slipped down remarkably well alongside the perfectly pink lamb. At some point, she noted with vague interest that all three bottles had been decanted and finished. The evening was balmy, and despite Jess' bawdy musings, Evelyn's shoulders remained perfectly warm. Angus had his shirt-sleeves rolled up as usual, and she found herself stealing increasingly frequent glances at his forearms. She was trying not to make eye contact with him too often; she didn't trust herself to behave naturally with Jess' beady eyes on her. And yet she craved a hit of his expressive face, warm hazel eyes and easy, generous smile. Seb had taken the veneers possibly too far; it should have been a clue for her. Angus' teeth were lovely, but they looked like they were his own.

As she took the dinner plates back inside, she stuck her head around the den. One of the Harry Potter movies was playing loudly. Eddie looked sleepy; he was cuddling Charlie on the sofa while Mike and Mia had gravitated to the beanbags. Evelyn blew him a kiss.

Outside, Zoe was serving up milky panna cotta, scattered with poached rhubarb. It looked incredible. Angus was uncorking a small bottle of dessert wine. 'I asked Zoe what was for pudding, and brought along some Orange Muscat,' he explained. 'They should go nicely together.'

'We are bookending our meal with wine pairings from Angus,' observed Evelyn primly.

'I beg your pardon?' Jess squinted at her in confusion.

'Bookending. I learnt it from Zoe the other day. It's when you begin and end a meal with similar things.'

'Okay, but champagne and dessert wine are not similar.'

'No, but they're both from Angus...' Evelyn tailed off, aware she was making no sense.

'What else have you learnt from your stay, besides hogget and bookending?' asked Angus, turning in his chair and looking at her in amusement. He carefully poured out the dessert wine into some small glasses that had materialised from nowhere. Ooh, dessert wine was dangerously potent—she took a sip—and also absolutely delicious.

'I have learnt that it's not wise to marry someone who's gay—unless, of course, you are gay too; then it works well,' said Evelyn, graciously gesturing to Jess and Zoe. Jess cracked up.

'Also, I've learnt that I love being in nature, and I love the land, and I love learning about the land,' she finished inarticulately.

'*The things that we love tell us what we are*,' said Angus.

Evelyn stared at him. 'That's very profound.' She noticed him exchange a look with Zoe, and they both giggled.

'Oh, for fuck's sake, you pompous twats,' said Jess, digging into her panna cotta.

'Huh?' asked Evelyn. 'I don't get it.'

'That's not him talking; he's quoting someone,' explained Jess, gesturing at Angus with her spoon. 'Probably someone who's been dead for centuries.'

'Thomas Aquinas,' Zoe and Angus chorused in unison.

Jess rolled her eyes. 'Sadly, that sort of thing is very standard around here. Bullshit theologians, both of them.'

Evelyn giggled.

'Wow, is that the time?' asked Angus. He stretched his arms upwards and then let his right arm fall along the back of Evelyn's chair. She was leaning forward, so it didn't touch her back, but that didn't stop Jess from completely losing the plot. She dove forward, burying her head in her napkin, and proceeded to howl with laughter. Evelyn crossed her arms and glared at her. Angus and Zoe looked confused.

'Right,' said Jess, sitting up and catching Evelyn's look, 'I'm going to clear up.' She jumped up and scuttled off, sniggering to herself.

'My wife has officially lost it,' said Zoe, raising an eyebrow in a sexy way that Evelyn thought they must teach you in French high schools.

'I'd better be getting off,' said Evelyn reluctantly. She was loath to break up this dinner, but she was feeling tired and woozy, and poor little Eddie must be exhausted. She stumbled to her feet and headed through the garden room, an empty bottle in each hand. 'Eddie—' she called, and stopped at the threshold of the den. Charlie was curled up in a small black ball on the sofa, and wrapped around him, fast sleep, was Eddie. His mouth hung slackly open and one little golden arm was flung over the puppy. 'Oh my goodness,' she murmured. She softly called to the others. 'Come and look at this.'

They gathered round the door-frame.

'Oh bless them,' said Jess, who had managed to pull herself together. 'He can stay here tonight if you like, angel? We can carry him up to Mike's room.'

'No, it's ok thanks—he has tutoring in the morning; I'd rather he got a proper sleep,' said Evelyn. 'I'll just wake him up and he'll be back in bed at the cottage in five minutes.' Bugger. She hated to wake him when he was so sound asleep.

'If you're still at the cottages, then I can carry him back for you,' Angus offered. 'It'd be a shame to wake the little lad.'

'Oh goodness me, no, I can't ask you to do that. He's—he's deceptively heavy,' Evelyn stammered.

'Nonsense. It can't be more than three or four hundred yards. I can do that easily.'

'Thank you, Angus! That sounds like the perfect solution!' Jess beamed. '*Doesn't it*, Evie?'

GOODBYES SAID, they headed out of the house together, Charlie padding along beside them. Angus had put Eddie over his shoulder without the boy stirring at all and seemed to be bearing his dead weight easily. The night was warm, and the birds were still chirping. The air smelt of jasmine.

Evelyn was feeling flustered. Jess had practically shoved them out the door, looking positively thrilled at this development. She was holding Eddie's trainers, and the laces swung as she walked. Now that she was on the move, the alcohol was really hitting her. She couldn't think of anything articulate to say to Angus, and she didn't want to wake Eddie, so she stayed silent. Angus was quiet too, but he looked far more relaxed than she felt, a small smile playing on his lips.

'That was such a fun evening,' said Evelyn eventually. She didn't do silence particularly well. 'I can't remember the last time I laughed that much.'

'Me neither,' laughed Angus. 'Jess is such a character.'

'She really is. She's always been like that. Just incorrigible.'

'Thank you for bringing along that incredible wine.' Angus shifted Eddie's weight on his shoulder. 'It was such a treat. I definitely don't get to drink like that very often.'

'You mean in terms of quality, or quantity?'

'Both! Usually, they're inversely correlated. So it was very indulgent indeed to gorge ourselves on wine of that calibre.'

'I completely agree.' She did agree. It had felt amazing to let go, to open up such great bottles and share them with friends for no better reason than that it was a warm spring night and they were feeling convivial. She and Seb had a cellar full of stuff like that. Why didn't they get stuck in more often? What was the point of just hoarding all those cases, perfectly up-lit in their glass-fronted cellar so that important guests could fawn over them?

'There's more where that came from,' she added. 'I brought down a case of each. We must do it again.'

She was aware that that sounded flirtatious, but she didn't care. She felt emboldened by the wine and the dark.

'I can think of nothing nicer.' His voice was serious.

They'd reached the cottage. Evelyn opened the door. Housekeeping had been in to provide their turndown service, so the table lamps were on dimly.

Angus gestured with his free hand. 'Upstairs?' he whispered.

'Yes. Here, let me show you.'

She led him up the narrow stairs and into Eddie's little twin-bedded room. She pulled the duvet on his bed back further and picked up his bunny. As Angus lowered him down, Evelyn cupped Eddie's head and laid it gently on the pillow. He stirred and curled onto his side. She carefully tucked the bunny into the space between his arms and his chest and pulled his duvet up around his chin. Then, kissing him on the cheek, she turned out the bedside light.

Angus stood back, letting her get through the door, and followed her downstairs. His presence seemed to fill the room. She turned to him.

'Thank you so much for carrying him home,' she said softly. 'It was an incredibly sweet thing to do.'

He smiled at her. He looked a little wistful. 'It was no problem at all, and I hope you don't think I'm odd if I say that I quite enjoyed it. My boys are twenty and eighteen now. It goes so fast. I miss those days when they needed me. It's nice to think I can still be useful occasionally.'

'I'm sure they still need you more than they let on.' Evelyn rubbed the inner corner of her eye, trying not to smudge her makeup. That would be really attractive. 'That walk just reminded me there are some things that, as a woman, I just can't physically do. Like carry a sleeping eight-year-old that far. It looks as if my marriage is over, and I guess I'm going to be a single parent a lot of the time. I'll just have to get used to it.'

She looked around the room. Despite the soft lamp-light and the tasteful furnishings, it wasn't home, and she and Eddie were here alone, essentially in some kind of limbo. A rogue tear ran down her cheek, startling her.

'Oh God, sorry,' she stammered, mortified. She brushed it away.

Angus stepped forward. 'If you don't mind my saying, you look like you could use a good hug. May I?'

She caught his eye and nodded. He pulled her towards him and put his arms around her tightly, then he moved one hand and cupped the back of her head. She sank into him. She wasn't quite sure what she should do with her arms, so she wrapped them around his lower back. He was stockier than Seb; his back was solid and muscular. She laid her cheek against his chest, and felt the comforting, rhythmical beat of his heart. Her eyes were wet, and she was sure she was both leaking mascara onto his nice shirt and giving herself panda-eyes. She closed them. All of her senses were on high alert. Her meditation teacher would be proud, she thought—total presence, the holy grail of mindfulness. She inhaled his smell: earthiness, laundry liquid and skin. It was heaven.

She noticed that she was stroking his lower back in very, very small movements, as if by making them tiny enough, he might not notice them. He moved his hand from her head and started to rub her bare upper back, across from one shoulder to the other and back, rhythmically. The skin on his hand felt slightly rough, but in a nice way. The room was starting to sway. She opened her eyes to get her balance, and their pose felt even more intimate here, in this empty room, with her eyesight in play. She could see his chest rising and falling through his shirt. She had two thoughts simultaneously: ask him to stay, and you *cannot* do that. She pulled away, slightly, but enough. He unwrapped his arms. She stood back and stared at him.

'Jesus,' she managed, 'you're a good hugger.' Phew. She realised she'd been holding her breath.

The look in his eyes seemed to be somewhere between amused and aroused. He opened his mouth as if to say something and shut it again. He stepped forward, gently put his hands on her bare shoulders, and kissed the top of her head.

'Goodnight Evelyn,' he said. 'Sleep tight.'

19

The hangover was monstrous. Evelyn had forgotten that heavy reds always did that to her. At least she and Eddie had both slept until eight-thirty. Lord knew, they'd needed it. She couldn't remember the last time she'd slept that late.

She sometimes found it helpful to over-compensate when she had a hangover. Mind over matter. She could spend the day in misery, or she could fight it. Two of her effervescent alkalising tablets and a full face of makeup later, she felt slightly more human. There was only one thing for it. An enormous breakfast.

She and Eddie walked hand-in-hand to the Oast House. Thankfully, they were too late to risk bumping into Angus on his morning rounds. Last night had really shaken her. Although nothing had technically happened, those minutes in the cottage had been more meaningful than anything else she'd experienced recently. She remembered her rush of longing, and how close she'd come to just yielding to it and asking him to stay.

What would he have said, done? He was a perfect gentleman, and he seemed quite old-fashioned, in a good way. She guessed he would have gently, kindly, turned her down. From his perspective she probably seemed slightly unstable, her face was all over the tabloids, and Angus did not need that kind of upheaval in his nice, quiet life. And, of course, he may not have actually wanted her; it may have been all in her and Jess' heads, a schoolgirl fabrication when they should have known better. Well, thank God she'd held her tongue at any rate, and not made a total fool of herself by propositioning him. Still, she couldn't shake the memory of his hand rubbing her bare back. Back and forth. Skin on skin. She shivered. She wanted to experience more of his skin; his hands simply weren't enough.

At the Oast House, Eddie vacillated for a while between waffles and pancakes before plumping for the latter. Evelyn herself made what proved to be a spectacularly successful choice from the à la carte menu: a large slice of toasted rye bread topped with pesto, bacon, avocado, thinly sliced beef tomatoes, scrambled egg, and rocket. She wolfed it down with a cup of black coffee. Much better.

'You fell asleep with Charlie on the sofa last night,' she told Eddie, who was making impressive headway with his pancake stack.

'Did I?' He gave her a slow smile of wonder. 'Was Charlie asleep too?'

'Yup. You were both curled up together. It was adorable.'

'I don't remember going home.'

'Angus carried you. Over his shoulder, like a sack of potatoes.'

'Over his shoulder?!' Eddie looked ecstatic. 'That's so funny! Wow. He must be really strong.'

'Yes, he must be.' *He is strong; I felt those back muscles.* 'He's probably used to carrying baby calves around, so a little boy isn't going to present too much of a challenge. But you must thank him for the lift next time you see him. Do you like Charlie?'

'I love him! He's so cute, and he's really clever too. Mum, when can we get a puppy? I feel so happy when I'm with Charlie. Can we see him again today?'

Evelyn looked at him. There was a sticky patch of maple syrup at the side of his mouth. She wanted to kiss it off. His hair was sticking up on one side. Her little man. Soon, probably, he'd be her only man.

She had to admit, she'd been thinking of whether a puppy would be a suitable option for Eddie. If she and Seb got divorced, which was looking more and more likely, then a dog could be a wonderful source of comfort and security for him. His school had recently got a dog, and the email from Mr Whitlow had explained that dogs had been shown to provide children with critical emotional support. Given the school was a total hot-house, it was comforting to know that the kids received some kind of support for their mental health.

'It's something we can look into,' she told Eddie.

'*Really*? Really, Mummy? Oh my word!'

'What kind of dog do you think you'd like?'

'A spaniel. Definitely a spaniel. They're cuddly, but they're also really clever.'

'Well, let's start doing some research.' She reached over and popped a piece of Eddie's pancake in her mouth. Mmm. 'Maybe we can make a list of questions to ask Angus about Charlie.' She was aware that she was looking for excuses to say his name.

'That would be great! And we can do some research online too, can't we?'

Evelyn was about to answer, when a shadow fell over her. She looked up and found Gino standing by the table.

'What are you doing here?' She hadn't meant to sound so cold, but she was shocked to see him here. This was *her* space; he belonged in London, securely confined to her work life. Although he wasn't confined to work, of course; he had crept insidiously into her marriage.

'Hi Evelyn.' He was looking well—tanned and suave. 'I wanted to come down and talk to you, face to face.' He turned to Eddie. 'Hey, dude! I'm Gino.'

'Hey!' beamed Eddie. They high-fived.

Great, thought Evelyn. Another of her menfolk bewitched by Gino.

'Do you think we can speak?' Gino tugged awkwardly at the collar of his pale pink polo shirt. He glanced at Eddie and then back at Evelyn.

'Eddie, honey,' she said, 'do you want to take your book and read out the front for a bit? You've got half an hour till you need to be online with your teachers. I'll be able to see you through the windows.'

'Cool,' said Eddie, hopping off his seat. 'Can I sit in the swing-chair?'

'Of course you can.' Evelyn handed him his Dog Man book, and he ran off. She picked up his plate and stacked it on top of her own, gesturing for Gino to take his vacated seat.

'I'm sorry—it may be a bit... sticky over there.'

'No problem,' said Gino. He sat down, stretching out his long legs and crossing them at the ankles. He was, inevitably, wearing loafers with no socks. 'I'm sorry for turning up like this. The thing is—I couldn't bear the way things have been left between us, and I wanted to come down here and apologise to you face-to face.'

A waitress appeared to clear the plates, and Gino ordered a double espresso.

'No intermittent fasting today?' He raised an eyebrow.

'Definitely not,' said Evelyn. 'And I even had bread. I'm seriously hungover.'

Gino tutted. 'What would Seb say?'

Evelyn laughed, despite herself. 'Seb can go to hell.' They'd broken the tension.

'Evelyn.' He leant over and grabbed her hand. 'I'm truly sorry for my part in all this. I know that I must have caused you great pain. I have a huge amount of respect for you as a boss, and I'm very fond of you as a person. You've given me a wonderful opportunity at your company and I've betrayed you.'

Evelyn looked into his huge brown eyes and sighed. She tried unsuccessfully to extricate her hand. 'You're not really the problem, Gino. Seb is. I can't change the fact that he's gay, but his behaviour has been pretty shitty: ten years of lying to me and cheating on me. And then he takes up with a member of my team! It's not only hugely disrespectful to me, but it's an enormous abuse of his power where you are concerned.'

'Please don't worry about me, Evelyn. I can handle myself. And I deceived you as much as Seb did.'

'You did, but you're not my husband. And I do worry about you. You're involved with your ultimate boss. There are reasons why that's heavily discouraged. He's in a position of power, and you're not. I mean, this is what the whole MeToo movement centres on. What if he gets bored and finishes with you? Or what if you break up with him? You can't be sure that neither scenario will affect your career. There's such a monstrous conflict there. I don't doubt his feelings for you, but I am appalled that he's been so unprofessional about this.'

'You're right, of course.' Gino shrugged. 'I've come to the same conclusion myself. That's why I'm looking at other roles; I wanted to tell you in person.'

'Oh, no. I'm genuinely sorry to hear that.' Evelyn really was sorry. 'You're very good at your job. I feel like we've gelled well over the past few months—you seem to see our brand through the same lens that I do.'

'I love your brand. It's beautiful. I love you. But I also love your husband.' Gino threw his hands in the air. 'I agree with you; I cannot be with him and work for him. I also cannot expect you to have me reporting to you, when I've behaved in such a way. Seb is in denial about all this, which is why I need to take matters into my own hands. It may take a little while to find the right role, as it's been a very recent decision. But I'm guessing it's helpful for you to have me stick around while you're taking time out?'

'Yes, it is,' Evelyn admitted. She drained her coffee cup and took a breath.

'Gino? Tell me about you and Seb—your story, I mean. I don't know it.'

'Are you sure you want to hear it?'

'I am. I'd like to understand what's going on with you guys.' It might have been seeing Gino in the flesh, or the still-fresh memory of her evening with Angus, but her anger and hurt seemed to be giving way to curiosity and concern.

'Well, ok then.' Gino fiddled with his little espresso spoon. 'Its super-weird to be talking to you about this. But you deserve honesty. And I'm happy to tell you our story.

'I bumped into Seb at a discreet, stylish gay bar in Soho.

I think he was pretty panicked when he saw me. But we got talking, and I told him his secret was safe with me. I didn't stay long that evening.

'Then the next week at work, he messaged me and asked me if we could go for coffee. He was upset; he explained to me that hiding his sexuality was really getting to him. I got it —I'm from a super-religious family and it was hard for me to come out. He told me he'd been lying to you for so long and he didn't know how to stop. He really loves you.'

'So he says,' said Evelyn, 'and yet I don't think I even really know him.'

'He asked me if I would go out with him for a drink,' Gino continued. 'I was very uncomfortable—I found him super-attractive, but I really liked you and it was all a bit too closely connected, you know? With me working for you? But we went out, and... we knew it was serious pretty quickly; it wasn't some casual hook-up.

'I honestly don't know what would have happened if that paper hadn't got those photos. Seb was horrified, of course, but the timing was lucky; it took all his decisions right out of his hands. But I know that for you, it has been a nightmare, Evelyn. And for your little son. He's beautiful; he's so like Seb, no? The same eyes.'

'He is,' said Evelyn grimly. 'So what now for you guys?'

'Well, it's great between us right now—me and Seb, I mean. It will be better when I get a new job—more equal. And you? How are you doing?'

'I'll be ok. Eddie and I will both be ok. I'm not looking forward to getting back to work and having to interact with my husband, though.'

'It will be hard,' agreed Gino. 'But you are an amazing woman, and I hope you will find love again. You are far, far too beautiful to have a gay husband. It is such a waste. Come to Italy! Let me take you. The guys there will go crazy for you.'

Evelyn laughed. 'That sounds very appealing. Seb and I share an appreciation for Italian men. But I'm not sure I'm ready to be set up by my husband's boyfriend—that's a step too far for now.'

'Ok, ok, I'll be patient. But I hope you will be happy soon. I'd better get back to London. Carrie thinks I am at the dentist. *Ciao, bella.*'

20

That afternoon, while Eddie played tennis with Mike, Evelyn buried herself away on the mezzanine level of the Oast House to focus on the party planning. Another large black coffee in hand, she checked through the invitee list. Of the thirty journalists and influencers invited, she'd had five declines and only four acceptances. The rest hadn't bothered to reply. Rubbish, but typical. She was growing antsy; the event was three weeks away, and she was keen to lock in a good attendee list.

At least they'd confirmed the party-planner, Siobhan Quinn. Siobhan styled events for all the fashion and lifestyle industries' most desirable brands, and her taste was exquisite. She was due down to the farm on Monday to recce the site, but she and Evelyn were already enjoying a flurry of creative back-and-forth via WhatsApp and Pinterest. Evelyn knew they were on the same page regarding this event. Siobhan had sent her some heavenly suggestions for the floral displays and lighting, and she'd implied that one of London's dreamiest fashion labels might provide some of their beautiful chintzy cottons for the table linen. Not that that would be any good without the perfect list of attendees.

Her phone rang. It was Seb. She sighed and put in her earbuds. 'Hey.'

'Hi there!' He sounded jaunty. He was on the move somewhere. 'I hear you saw Gino this morning.'

'Yep. It was good of him to make the trip. What do you need?'

'Two things. Three, actually. I'm going to be on the cover of GQ next month! They pulled Daniel Craig.'

'That's fantastic. Impressive coup. Well done Carrie.'

'Indeed. Also, does the weekend after next suit for me to take Eddie down to Itchenor?'

'That should be fine.' She and Eddie had zero plans until the big party, and he'd love to see his dad.

'Thanks. Would you be cool if Gino joined us? I thought they could spend some time together.'

The thought of her son spending a weekend with his father and gay lover was so deeply bizarre that Evelyn couldn't even process it. Instead she said, 'That's fine, I guess. They met today, briefly, and seemed to hit it off. Just —please tread very carefully with him, Seb. It's a lot to get his little head around.'

'Yes, Gino mentioned it. That gave me the idea. We'll keep things very light-hearted and fun, I promise. And on the subject of Gino... darling, how would you feel about me going public with my relationship with him?'

Evelyn slammed down her coffee cup, sloshing the liquid into the saucer. For fuck's sake. She tried to mop it up with a tiny paper napkin. Seriously? The ink on the *Post's* article was barely dry; it hadn't even been two weeks. She wondered if this was some ploy by Seb to perpetuate the media cycle, which seemed to be drying up. Sales were slowly normalising to pre-bombshell levels. But then she thought, fuck it. It didn't matter whether Seb conducted his relationship publicly or privately. It wasn't actually any of her business.

'I guess that's fine,' she managed.

'Really?'

'Really. Are you going to give someone an exclusive?'

'No.' Seb sighed. 'This time I'm doing it on my terms, on my Instagram account. I'm riding high at the moment, Ev. There's still so much goodwill for me. And I'd rather control this narrative than have the paps following me and Gino around, trying to out us. I'll probably do it tomorrow.'

'Well, that sounds sensible. Good luck with it. I'll try to re-post it and say something supportive.'

'Jesus, Ev, you are a fucking angel. You know that, don't you? The way you've handled this... it's just amazing. I'm so lucky to have you in my life.'

'Seb. We need to have a very long chat at some point about... about next steps, and dissolving this marriage, and my future at the company.'

Seb's voice was soft. 'I know we do. And we can talk whenever you're ready. We should do it in person. But whatever happens to our relationship, we built this brand *together*, Ev. It's *ours*. Don't forget that. I want you back where you belong, by my side. It's time to come back to London.'

'I'm not coming back yet. I am working hard from here; I'm committed to the company. But you have to respect my need for space, Seb. In the space of two weeks, you've come out to me and the world and now you're publicly introducing your... boyfriend into the mix. It's humiliating. So let me hide down here for a few more weeks. Ok?'

She heard him sigh. 'Ok. It's the least I can do—I definitely owe you one.'

That was when she had a lightbulb moment. 'You do owe me one. In fact, it's going to take a lot to make up for ten years of lies. What are you doing the first Friday in July?'

THE LACTIC-ACID PHASE of the hangover was kicking in, and Evelyn's legs ached. She needed to run this out. She packed up her laptop and headed back to the cottage. She had no specific running gear with her, but her yoga stuff would do. She switched her dress for a crop top, leggings and trainers. It was warm, but at least she could sweat out the booze effectively. She picked an upbeat playlist on Spotify and turned up the volume.

Grabbing a water-bottle, Evelyn set off at a steady pace, starting along the road that led to Sorrel Farm and then cutting through a pretty field.

As she ran, the music pumping, she felt that old rush of exhilaration that she first discovered while doing cross-country at school. No matter what the weather, running took her out of her body and made her soul soar. It was as though she was looking down on herself, and on the gently swaying fields of crops. She knew it was a purely chemical reaction as her brain orchestrated its blessed dopamine release, but it felt spiritual. The cramping in her legs was easing, and she felt a vast rush of wellbeing.

Yes, her marriage had ended. Yes, tomorrow Seb would show the world that the commitments they'd made to each other in the *Post* interview were in fact total bullshit, and that he had a young, handsome, male lover. Yes, she was effectively sidelined, in her marriage and most likely in the social circles that they moved in, for who wants a rejected wife around the dinner table when you can have the newest, hottest, most charismatic gay couple in town?

But in that moment, she didn't really care. The dinner party circuit, their gleaming white offices, even her beautifully curated home—none of it seemed real right now. Reality in this moment was the baked clay beneath her feet, the melodic chorus of songbirds, the smell of fresh growth that surrounded her, and the warmth of the sun. She was in a bubble; she knew that, but she felt cocooned within its gentle confines.

After five kilometres of running through hot fields and sweetly damp woods, Evelyn turned back and retraced her steps, coming off the road early. If she was correct, this path should bring her around the back of the farm.

One stile later, she came to the Sorrel Farm lavender fields. She slowed down in amazement. The long rows of lavender were nearing full bloom, and countless puffs of bluish purple surrounded her. The sight and smell were intoxicating. She took a gulp from her water bottle and bent down, picking a stem and rubbing the flowers between her fingers to release the scent. How had she not been over here yet? She must show Eddie; he'd love it. Oh, it was heaven.

There was a small group of men working on the other side of the field. One of them waved at her. It was Angus! Her heart leapt. Shit. Her skin and hair were dripping with sweat. He was walking over. She walked to meet him.

'Hi, Angus,' she managed. He was wearing a fitted white polo shirt with Sorrel Farm branding and beige shorts. His legs were muscular and deeply tanned. The shirt showed his arms off perfectly; it appeared as though his biceps were just as worthy of her attention as his forearms. Oh, sweet Jesus. But none of it could compete with his face. Dear lord, that face. How was it that every time she looked at him, he became more gorgeous?

He was even wearing aviators. For God's sake. Evelyn was of the generation of women who had been ruthlessly conditioned to equate aviators with Tom Cruise in *Top Gun*, and therefore with raw, male sex appeal.

'Hello.' He raised his aviators onto his head and smiled his delectable, crinkly smile at her, nodding at her running gear. 'Impressive.'

'Ha, thanks. I needed to flush out the hangover. It seems I was very thirsty last night.'

He laughed. 'We all were. It was hard not to be thirsty with such incredible wine flowing. Thank you again for spoiling us.'

Evelyn was embarrassed. 'Jess and Zoe did most of the spoiling. But this place is idyllic—I had no idea the lavender was already out or I would have come over here sooner.' She took a swig from her bottle and wiped her mouth.

'It's getting there. We've got another few weeks before we harvest it, thankfully. I could never tire of this sight.' He cast his eyes around the sweeping belt of colour. 'I saw you this morning in the Oast House—you looked deep in conversation.'

Hmm. So he'd clocked her? That was encouraging. 'Oh, really? Well, Eddie and I had a very intense chat about whose breakfast was better, but if it wasn't Eddie you saw me with, then it must have been Gino. He's a—colleague, who came down from London to talk to me.'

'Ah.'

'He's also my husband's new boyfriend.'

'Shit.' Angus looked startled. 'I wasn't expecting that. Are you ok? Your husband and your colleague? Isn't that a little—off?'

'It's a lot off. But you know what, I'm more ok with it than I thought I would be. And I'll give you a world exclusive. They're going public with their relationship tomorrow.'

'*Evelyn*. I'm so sorry.' Angus took a step towards her and shook his head. 'This must be such a tough time for you. You deserve to catch a break.'

She looked at him, watching her with concern and kindness and something else, and she drank him in. She didn't know if it was the endorphin rush from the run, or the enchanting purple haze that surrounded them, or the way he'd said her name.

She was frigging exhausted.

She was revoltingly sweaty.

She was stone-cold sober.

But he was looking at her in a such a way that she felt as though she could take flight.

Fuck it.

'Angus,' she said. Her voice was clear. 'I think I'm going to need another one of those hugs.'

21

'You what?' Jess was staring at her in amazement.

'We hug.'

'What on earth do you mean, you hug?'

It was Friday, and she and Jess were having drinks together at the Oast House. Eddie had gone down to the south coast with Seb and Gino that morning. He'd been bursting with excitement when they picked him up for their boys' trip. It sounded as though Seb had secured a gorgeous pad with a pool down in Itchenor, and, judging from the photos he'd sent through, Eddie was having a ball. His absence afforded her the first opportunity to catch up properly with Jess since their boozy dinner on Tuesday. Zoe had taken a break from the kitchen and was having a glass of wine with them while in her chef's whites.

Evelyn attempted to clarify. 'Well, we came downstairs the other night in the cottage after Angus got Eddie into bed, and I was a bit emotional, so he offered to hug me. And then we just stood there, embracing each other, for—I don't know—a minute?

'Then I bumped into him the next day, at the end of my

run. It was right after Seb had told me he was going public with Gino, and I asked him to hug me again. And he did. Right in the middle of your lavender field.'

'Right,' said Jess. 'I need far, far more information.' She leant in. 'Describe exactly what these hugs were like. Would you say they were friendly?'

'Um,' Evelyn shifted in her seat, 'not friendly, exactly.'

'You mean unfriendly, or they were more than friendly?'

'More than friendly. They were very intense, and... tender.'

Jess did one of those closed-mouth, silent laughs that came out through her nose like a sharp exhalation. 'So you're telling me you've been sharing intense, lengthy, *tender* hugs with my delicious farm manager, but nothing more has happened?'

'Yes. No. Nothing has happened, unfortunately.'

'But you want it to?'

Evelyn could feel the heat rising up her face. 'Yes, I want it to. I'm—I'm not sure how to go about it though. My pickup skills are very rusty.'

'Oh, I'm not done with the questions. So you were both fairly hammered on Tuesday, right?'

'Oh yeah. Completely so.'

'But yesterday, you just hugged—embraced—him in the middle of a field, in broad daylight?'

Evelyn grinned. 'Yes. And I was so sweaty, I can't even tell you. I felt bad for the guy.'

Jess threw her hands up in exasperation. 'So, a pretty great way to kick things up a gear would have been to say, 'Hey Angus, I need to take a long, steamy shower. Want to give me a hand?' Don't you think?'

Zoe snorted.

Evelyn buried her face in her hands. 'You are excruciating. I'm not planning on behaving like I'm in some soft-porn movie, Jess. Now, do you have anything that would constitute useful advice?'

Jess turned to Zoe. 'What do you think, my love?'

'I think,' Zoe said, nodding slowly, 'that this is super, super sexy. It's the hottest thing I've ever heard.'

'I totally agree,' said Jess. 'It's so *Victorian*. I love it. Ok, tell us more.'

'Well,' Evelyn began, 'the other night, it almost scared me. The intensity of feeling, I mean, and being alone with him like that when nothing at all had happened between us before. And when it was over, he just put his hands on my shoulders and kissed the top of my head, and he said 'Goodnight, Evelyn' and left.'

'Ooh!' Jess drummed her fists on the table. 'God. He really is a brooding hero, isn't he? Dear, reliable Angus, out toiling on the land day after day—who knew he had these depths of intensity? And what about yesterday?'

'Yesterday was even better. It seemed more relaxed, like we were a little more comfortable with each other. But it was incredible, just being wrapped up in his arms, under the sun, with that wonderful lavender all around us. It felt like the earth was moving, to be honest, like—your term, Zoe—a *communion*.'

When she asked him her favour, his face broke out into a grin so broad that it made her laugh in delight and relief. He reached her in a single stride and wrapped his arms around her, even more tightly than before, as if emboldened by her invitation. He pressed one palm between her shoulder blades, and the other caressed the slippery, bare small of her back. She kept her arms free this time, and they encircled his neck. She buried her face in his chest and breathed in the scent of his sweat, and of the lavender crops. They stayed there until they heard wolf-

whistling, which Evelyn realised to her mortification was coming from the men working on the field. Angus gently broke away from her, laughing.

'I suspect we've made their day,' he said. 'I'll never hear the end of it. I'd better go and remind them that we're here to work.' He kissed her on the cheek. 'You are also very good at hugging, Evelyn Macleod,' he whispered.

She jogged off, face aflame and heart singing.

'Well, that sounds like a religious experience to me,' marvelled Jess. 'You lucky cow. Can you imagine what it'll be like when you actually shag him? Celestial choirs will break out in song...'

'Don't.' Evelyn held up a hand. 'I can't even think about it in case it never happens. Shit, girls. I feel like a teenager. What should I do?'

'I would be pleased to talk to him, Evie.' Zoe reached over and put a hand on top of Evelyn's. 'I am so fond of you both. He is an exceptional guy. But he's shy, like you. He had a nasty divorce. I don't think he's the kind of person to rush into anything, or have a casual fling. He hasn't really dated since Audrey divorced him.'

Angus and Audrey. How alliterative. Evelyn irrationally imagined an Audrey Hepburn doppelgänger, poised and immaculate. She let out a deep sigh and put her wineglass to her lips. 'Thank you, Zoe. You're an angel. But I won't ask you to do that. I'm too old to play games, getting my friends to find out if a guy likes me. I don't want to scare him off. I shall just try to be patient and let things take their natural course. I have a pretty crazy few weeks ahead in any case, with the party and this meeting with our investor—I seriously need to pull my finger out and show him I'm committed to the company. He's a bit of a jackass, and he's very sceptical that Seb and I can rise above our personal problems and work together effectively.'

'And can you?' asked Jess. 'How are you feeling about going back?'

'Conflicted,' admitted Evelyn. 'I guess that's a good reason to exercise some self control where Angus is concerned. I'll be back in London in a few weeks, trying to make things work in my new reality. It's a scary thought, but I am looking forward to getting back into the thick of it at work. I'll be able to do far more schmoozing when I'm based back in London, and Seb and I are brilliant together at work—it's the best part of our relationship, to be honest. You know we've always riffed off each other so well. I miss our banter and our brainstorming chats.'

Jess nodded. 'Well, if you can get out of the marriage smoothly and keep the business relationship intact, then major kudos to you, sweetie. I hope he is beyond fucking grateful to you. You've given him a seriously easy time of it.'

'On that note.' Evelyn perked up. 'I have a surprise for you. I hope it's a good one. The invitations for the party haven't been going well—we were getting very few acceptances, and I was pretty worried. I really want to get a killer attendee list for you. So I called in a favour from Seb. Much as it pains me to say it, he's a far bigger draw than me. His social following is huge, and he's flying very high right now. Everyone wants a piece of him, and now that he and Gino have gone public, they'll be the toast of London. Seb's Instagram post introducing Gino as his boyfriend has had a million likes in the last forty-eight hours. A million! Insane.' Evelyn shook her head in disbelief.

'The point is, Seb will come. To the party. He's willing to attend in whatever capacity we want. He can come as a guest, he can host it, he can do an endearing speech where he waxes lyrical about how Sorrel Farm is his favourite bolt-hole. Whatever. He can even announce some kind of collaboration with you guys. The company is still sourcing far too much of its food from continental Europe. If you want to deepen the relationship between the farm and the resort in all of your marketing, this would be a wonderful way to tie the two sides together. Imagine the walled garden full of guests. They're soaking up the unique ambiance of this place, and they're listening to Seb announcing that Sorrel Farm is now a preferred supplier for Seb Macleod Ltd, because of his commitment to supporting organic and biodynamic producers.' She paused for breath. 'What do you think?'

Zoe and Jess looked at each other.

'What I want to do,' said Jess, 'is to tell Seb to stay the fuck away from our farm. I'm so fucking angry with the way he's treated you. Are you sure you could handle having him swanning around here for a whole evening?'

'I promise, I'm fine with it. I think it's too good an opportunity to miss. This is playing right into Seb's strengths, for *your* gain.'

'In that case—this is big, Evie. Not just the draw of having him come here and pull in all those glamorous, influential people that we need so badly, but the collaboration on the sourcing side. Do you seriously think that's an option? If so, I could be persuaded to be civil.'

'Of course it is, and I'm kicking myself that I've never done this before,' said Evelyn. 'Zoe, what's your gut reaction?'

'I agree, this could be huge for us,' said Zoe slowly. 'We'd have to sit down with Angus and look at our potential capacity across crops, livestock and the walled garden produce. As you know, our ramp-up plans won't happen overnight.'

'Excellent,' said Evelyn. 'I'm so happy you're on board in theory. I can email our sourcing team and see what kind of quantities we get through at the moment—I have no idea off the top of my head. This is exciting, ladies! Now, to go back to the party. What do you say Seb hosts it? An Evening with Seb Macleod at Sorrel Farm. I can't think of a single journalist who won't drop everything to attend. It'll be the hottest, most exclusive ticket of summer. We can get Gino along too—it's an extra pull for the press, and it's free social media for us. He can generate gorgeous content for your social channels but also for Seb's; that way you'll pick up a ton of extra followers.'

'I'm in.' Jess pulled the bottle of Sancerre out of the bucket by the table and refilled their glasses. 'This takes us to the next level, ladies.'

'Hurrah!' Evelyn drank up. 'I'll start calling around first thing Monday morning. Siobhan is due Monday afternoon to recce the walled garden. Let's thrash the rest of it out on Tuesday. Sorrel Farm is about to hit the map. I hope you're ready.'

22

The heatwave was still going strong. This would surely be the hottest June on record. Jess had procured a table and parasol in a blessedly shady corner of the walled garden. They meant business. This was a working lunch; there was no wine to steer them off-course. Instead, carafes of iced water dotted the table, twisting ribbons of cucumber suspended within. Zoe had organised a large mezze platter piled high with crudites and rare-breed cured meats from the farm, as well as still-warm flat-breads and creamy, pine-nut-topped houmous.

Evelyn was attempting to get into business mode. She'd dressed the part in an immaculate white cotton shirt-waister dress cinched with a wide, tan leather belt. Her hair was freshly blow-dried, and she'd even put in her enormous diamond studs—her fuck-off diamonds, as Jess called them. But there was the matter of Angus sitting opposite her, being perfectly pleasant, perfectly polite, perfectly friendly, as if he'd never held her face to his heart, or stroked the skin between her shoulder-blades. She took a sip of water and breathed. If he could be businesslike, so could she.

'Before we get into the sourcing side of things, do you want to give us an update on the party, Evie?' prompted Jess, munching on a flatbread. 'Did you manage to call around the invitees yesterday?'

Evelyn grinned. 'Believe me, I didn't have to. I emailed most of the reworked invitations out on Saturday, with Seb's name in the title. By Sunday, I had a full quota of acceptances. Marjorie Lonsdale is coming, which I'm thrilled about. She's the biggest lifestyle blogger in the UK and her photography is wonderful. She's asked if she can bring her own photographer—I said it was fine. The greatest coup is Arianna Rodriguez, who's flying herself over from Houston, Texas for a long weekend.'

'Who is she?' enquired Angus. 'I'm afraid I'm not familiar.'

'Don't worry; I'm not sure you're her target follower,' Evelyn laughed. 'Arianna has even more Instagram followers than Seb—five million, last time I checked. She's a huge, huge US lifestyle blogger; she does everything from fashion to wellness and interiors. I invited her on a whim: she's well-known for being a huge Anglophile. She's obsessed by the royals, by English culture. She's always reposting photos of rose-clad rectories and cream teas, and her followers go mad for them. If we want to put this place on the map, we should get more US visitors over here. They all go straight to the Cotswolds; we need to show them what an easy destination Kent is if they fly into London. Seb will definitely help us on that front too; he has a huge US following.'

'That sounds fantastic, Evie,' said Zoe. 'Great work.'

'We've got a good line-up of journalists attending too,' Evelyn continued. 'The Sunday supplements, *Harper's Bazaar*, *Conde Nast Traveller*, and some broadsheets. That woman from the *Tribune*, Sadie Thomas, is among them. Oh, and *Food* magazine's agreed to come too. It transpires that Seb coming out while we were on their magazine cover really boosted their sales. I've promised them a sit-down with him and also with you guys. We should discuss the exact angle, but it'll be great exposure for the amazing work you're doing on the farm. They've got the Organic Issue coming up so we can push to be part of that.'

She looked up. Angus was gazing at her appreciatively. He'd never seen her in full-on work mode, she realised. She probably just came across as a wealthy lady of leisure. What was the term they'd coined in *Dirty Dancing* for those women who stayed on at Kellerman's while their husbands worked? Bungalow bunnies. She'd done a pretty good impression of a bungalow bunny since she'd been here.

She smiled at him. Galvanised, she continued. 'Do you want a quick update on the meeting with Siobhan yesterday? Siobhan is our party planner,' she told Angus.

'Please,' said Jess. 'That's why I thought it would be helpful to have this meeting here, so that we can visualise it.'

'Ok,' said Evelyn, looking down at the notes on her MacBook. 'This is the most exciting part, for me—dressing this place so that the guests feel like they've walked into the middle of *A Midsummer Night's Dream*. It's going to be amazing. Siobhan was blown away. She said it's a dream venue that will style itself.

'Because it will still be daylight when we eat, she suggests keeping the table-settings very fresh rather than making them too formal. She loves our idea of a single, long table running between the pool and the planting beds. It's very chic to do a single table—it looks incredible on Instagram when you take a photo from one end.

'We've opted for a green and white base for the colour

palette, punctuated by blues and purples to complement your herbaceous borders here in the garden. Siobhan works with wonderful florists whose style is very organic. They can create the flower arrangements for the tables, and also bring in planters and pots of the same flowers and plants—delphiniums, hydrangeas, ranunculus, roses, sweet-pea, mint, eucalyptus... it will smell insane, that's for sure. It should be such a beautiful sensory experience for the guests.'

'You're a genius, my angel.' Jess leaned over and kissed Evelyn on the cheek. 'An absolute genius. I can't believe you've pulled all this together so quickly.'

INEVITABLY, half an hour later Jess requested a bottle of rosé from a passing waitress as they looked through the numbers. Eloise in the procurement team had sent Evelyn through the quantities of fruit, vegetables, beef, lamb, pork, chicken, milk and eggs that the company ordered on a weekly basis.

'Here's how it breaks down.' Evelyn handed around some print-outs. 'Our restaurant, Seb's Kitchen, has the most regular consumption, but it's not enormous. Then we have our events on the line below—Seb usually does one big one a week; they're mostly corporate, often five hundred guests or more. The other opportunity is on the ecommerce side. Right now we mainly supply non-perishables like supplements and health foods, but we're looking to increase our fresh food offering beyond just our bottled juices and smoothies. That could be a fantastic opportunity for us to act as an affiliate and distribute anything from veg boxes to meat and eggs for you. It's also something we could have a lot of fun with—Seb is very focused on cooking with seasonal produce, just like you, so we could offer boxes of your produce based on his recipes. The recipe box sector has really taken off in the last couple of years.' She took a sip of her wine.

'Am I right in thinking,' asked Angus, pouring over the sheet, 'that you get through an enormous amount of eggs, and not much milk?'

'It's so funny you spotted that,' laughed Evelyn. 'You've got it in one. So take our café, for example; everyone goes there for scrambled egg and avocado, and we don't really use dairy. The ladies of west London are far too busy with their oat or almond milk. We use a bit, for kefir especially, but our requirements are pretty low.'

'We can help on the egg front if that's of interest,' replied Angus, looking over at Zoe. 'We've had plenty of discussions about increasing our population of laying hens, haven't we, Zo? It's easy to do from an infrastructure perspective, and we have the space.'

'Your eggs are delicious,' said Evelyn, as Zoe nodded. 'I've enjoyed them pretty much every morning since I've been here.' She patted her stomach, which was certainly protruding more than it had when she'd arrived in Kent.

'It always comes back to the same issue.' Jess leaned forward. 'Capital allocation. Where's the biggest opportunity, where should we be spending our money, and where else can we dial down spending to fund that? Perhaps with a clear idea from Seb and Evelyn of where their interests lie, we can do some number-crunching on whether we're investing in the highest-demand areas.'

'Don't forget, not all the spending will yield an immediate return,' warned Angus. 'Yes, there are some areas that we can ramp up quickly, like the overflow kitchen garden out the back there. But all the investment in developing the soil for biodynamic farming—that's a slow-burn, at least at first.'

'We believe it will pay dividends when it's all set up,' Zoe confirmed, 'and it will yield a more premium product, but it's a long-term investment.'

Evelyn nodded. 'I know things have been... slow on the resort side recently. Is raising additional capital to fund some of this an option at all?'

Jess and Zoe exchanged glances. 'We're old-fashioned,' said Jess matter-of-factly. 'My parents were risk averse, and we've run things the same way. We have a credit line from the bank that's big enough to keep us up at night, and that's it. No equity investors. We fund everything else through the sales this place generates.'

'Well, that's very laudable, and a sound position to be in,' Evelyn pointed out. 'If it's something you ever want to consider, then Seb and I have had a lot of experience of raising money over the last few years, and we can guide you through the process. It's a bit of a minefield and it's always worth waiting for the right equity partner. Our current investor is a total dick. He's getting us in for a meeting next week—he's making things difficult for me. The problem is that he's convinced that Seb and I won't be able to co-run the company properly once we've divorced. Seb called me this morning to warn me. We're expecting him to try to give me the boot next week, unless I can deliver a hell of a pitch on why I should stay.'

'Oh my goodness!' gasped Jess. 'What a fucking snake. Surely he can't do that, can he? Don't you have a board, or something?'

'We do,' sighed Evelyn, 'but unfortunately Iguana—that's the investor—controls sixty percent of the voting shares, so they have the majority necessary to remove me as a director. They can't make me give up my shares, but they can force me to step down as an executive.'

'That's terrible, Evie. I'm so sorry.' Zoe refilled Evelyn's glass. 'Can you and Seb unite and fight him?'

'Sadly not. Seb owns seventeen percent of the company, and I own thirteen percent. The last ten percent is employee-owned. It's unusual for a married couple to have their stakes separated, but we chose this structure to reflect the fact that we both have C-suite positions in the company.'

'At least it'll make things more straightforward in the divorce.' Jess shrugged her shoulders.'

'Jess!' Evelyn laughed. 'You're outrageous. But right, as always.'

'Wait. I'm trying to do some maths in my head.' Jess was counting on her fingers. 'What did the company get valued at in your latest round? Two hundred million?'

Evelyn glared at her. 'Something like that.'

Jess whipped out her phone. 'Thirteen percent of a two hundred million is…' She gasped and hugged her phone to her chest. 'Fucking hell, Evie.'

'Let's move on, Jess.' Evelyn's face was crimson.

'Sorry, sorry. Very crass of me.'

'Evelyn, I'm sorry you're under such pressure,' said Angus, holding up his glass to her. 'Here's to you wiping the floor with them next week. We all have faith in you.'

'What can we do to help you?' asked Zoe, looking concerned.

'Just being here with you guys helps.' There was no reason Angus had to know the extent to which she included him in that sentiment. 'I do have one idea I'd like to raise. I've been thinking about it a lot this week.'

'What's that?' asked Zoe.

'You. As the face of the Sorrel Farm brand. Both of you, of course, but particularly Zoe, as the chef. This is such a special place, guys. Think about other destination restaurants: Daylesford, *La Petite Ferme* in Franschhoek, *Chez Panisse* in California. They all have a sense of place. I have all their cookbooks, because it's my way of conjuring up a little of their magic, even when I'm in London. You may take it for granted, but Sorrel Farm is heaven, and when all those people get down here in a couple of weeks, they're going to want a way to take a little piece of that heaven back home. And so will everyone else who comes to stay, especially as they become more familiar with your farm-to-table format. You're both gorgeous—and you're gay, which is so much chicer than a straight couple running it. This is gold-dust, I promise you. I want a Sorrel Farm cookbook, and I won't rest until I get it.'

23

The bustling reality of the Arts Club on Dover Street hit Evelyn as she entered the ground floor brasserie. It was a shock to be thrust back into the beating heart of London. When she was in Kent, London felt to her like an amorphous haze. She'd gone underground for a few weeks, but London had continued to throb and pulse and flourish without her.

She wasn't quite ready to be back here full time, but she was startled by the rush of vitality that she felt when she stepped through the Arts Club's familiar black doors. She wasn't a member; it was a bit too corporate, too power-hungry for her (although Seb loved that vibe), but she always enjoyed the infectious energy in this room as financiers and CEOs thrashed out deals against the back-drop of Georgian architecture and impressive contemporary art. She'd taken the train up from Kent so she could enjoy a glass of wine at lunch. It would be a fleeting trip before she returned to Eddie back at the farm.

She followed the host across the black-and-white tiled floor to a round table for four in the middle of the room.

The others were already seated. No one else could have got her back to London this soon, but she wouldn't miss this meeting for the world.

At the table were three of her favourite women on the planet, friends so dear and loyal and familiar that it felt as though they could read her mind. Evelyn was extremely judicious when it came to her social circle in London. She endured a great deal of fawning networking events for Seb's sake, and she largely shunned the Notting Hill school mums and their endless brunches, but these girls were different. She'd met them all through professional women's affinity networks over the years, and their relationships had grown deeper as their careers grew. The women in front of her were serious power-players in their industries. They regularly acted as a sounding board for each other, providing encouragement and demanding accountability, and helping each other to climb the slippery, wearisome ladder that was corporate success. When Evelyn had mentioned Ed Chang's sinister manoeuvres on their WhatsApp group chat, they'd declared that an emergency lunch was necessary.

'Evelyn Macleod! Get over here!' Stacey Fisher was the first to spot her. A glossy blonde American, Stacey had arrived in the UK years ago to assume her Rhodes Scholarship, and never left. She'd had an illustrious career in hedge funds before starting up her own FinTech firm. While Evelyn could never really have articulated what Stacey's company actually did, she found her and her achievements hugely impressive. That Stacey had four kids and an adoring husband was almost a given.

Stacey hugged her. 'You gorgeous creature! You are looking so fabulous! I *need* those pants. Are they Gabriela Hearst?'

'Spot on.' Evelyn laughed, kissing her. Stacey's fashion

radar was impeccable. She looked down at her trousers, which were beautifully tailored and cut from ice-blue wool crepe. They fell right to the bottom of her beige stiletto heels, performing a wonderful feat of elongation on her legs. 'I just had them sent over from Matches. I had nothing with me in Kent that would be fabulous enough for you, Stacey.'

'I'm on it. I hope they have them in my size.'

Evelyn turned to greet Nira. Nira Banerjee ran a British biotech firm that had recently been snapped up by a major US pharmaceuticals company for over a billion pounds. Their focus on anti-ageing drugs had, it turned out, been attractive to many parties. She was still running the biotech side as a standalone entity.

'Dear Nira,' said Evelyn, hugging her tightly. 'I'm so happy to see you.'

'My little Evelyn,' the other woman replied warmly. 'How are you doing, my dear?' She was taller than Evelyn, with a glossy blow-dry, and she was dressed in a stunning embellished shift that Evelyn recognised as current-season Prada.

The final woman at the table was older than the others by at least a decade, although she wore it well. The *Wall Street Journal* had described her as Margaret Thatcher crossed with Charlotte Rampling, and Evelyn suspected that Elaine Williams wore her steely reputation as a badge of honour. To those closest to her, however, she was always kind and unfailingly generous. Her onetime-boutique drinks company was now a sizeable conglomerate, thanks to a series of highly successful acquisitions in the world of artisanal spirits. She was also a long-time board member of Seb Macleod Ltd.

She kissed Evelyn on both cheeks and squeezed her hands. 'It is very good to see you, darling.'

As they took their seats, Evelyn noticed four mimosas on the table and a bottle of something chilling in the wine-cooler next to them. Stacey hadn't wasted any time.

'Important stuff first, before we get onto your plan for professional domination,' said Nira firmly. 'How are *you* doing? Seb's clearly just dandy with his delicious new boyfriend. I swear to God, that man is like a fucking rubber duck: nothing can keep him down.'

'He was born lucky,' laughed Evelyn. 'And it's all panned out brilliantly for him. I'm ok, I guess. I've been hiding out in Kent for the last few weeks, as I mentioned. It's actually been a very restorative time, and it got Eddie away from the paps and from the pressures of school which has been great for him.'

'That school is a freaking nightmare.' Stacey shook her head sagely. 'All they care about is getting as many boys as possible into St Paul's or Westminster. Woe betide you if you're not that kind of kid. You should really consider the American school. It may be a bit more Kum Ba Yah, but they get the results without fucking the kids up for life.'

'It could be something to think about for next term,' agreed Evelyn, 'though the headmaster has been terrific about this whole situation.'

'When are you coming back?' asked Stacey. 'There are so many guys we can fix you up with. You are going to have so much fun on the circuit. Now, ladies, are we thinking Evelyn should go older or younger?'

'I see you with a silver fox,' said Elaine confidently. 'You know the type—sold his hedge fund, kids are grown up, spends most of his time at his house in Cap d'Antibes or pottering around the Med on his yacht. You need a proper grown-up now, Evelyn. We all love Seb, but it must have been like having two kids, at times.'

Evelyn creased up. 'That's not far wrong.'

'Oh no, I think you should go younger, at least for a fling.' Nira finished off her mimosa and broke a breadstick in half. 'Come on, be a cliché for a while. Being a cliché is *so* much fun. I'm thinking tennis coach, personal trainer... biceps rather than brains. You've had ten years with a gay husband, darling. You need a nice, buff young man to show you what you've been missing.'

Evelyn's face was getting hot. 'Wow, ladies, I hadn't appreciated what a smorgasbord of options awaited me. You know, there is someone already, in Kent, but it doesn't look like it's workable, unfortunately.'

Stacey put her elbows on the table and leaned forward. 'Tell. Us. Now.'

'He's the farm manager of the farm and resort my friend runs. Sorrel Farm. His name is Angus. He's probably six or seven years older than me, divorced. He's very, very handsome and kind. And he was a theology scholar; he goes around sexily quoting Thomas Aquinas...' She shrugged her shoulders. 'But I'm back in London as of next week and he doesn't strike me as the type of guy who does casual flings. That's not what I want from him, anyway.'

The others looked at each other with raised eyebrows.

Stacey got in first. 'Wow. That is *fast* work, baby. He sounds smoking hot. I love your style.'

'Someone,' said Nira, 'sounds pretty smitten to me. Kent's like an hour from London. Can't you just make it work?'

'I dunno,' demurred Evelyn. 'I'm not sure he'd have much interest in the life I lead in London, somehow.'

Next to them, two bankers were indulging in some

mutual back-slapping while they loudly ordered a bottle of Cristal. Angus would absolutely detest this place, she thought.

'It sounds as if you've had a delightful time in Kent, with charming farmers and what looks like a bit of sunbathing,' said Elaine kindly. 'What's the name of the place you've been staying, again?'

'Sorrel Farm.' Evelyn pulled out her phone. 'Let me show you guys some photos. Honestly, this place is magical. My friend runs it with her wife. It's her old family farm, and they've turned the entire place over to organic farming, and now they're in the process of making it biodynamic. They have everything from lavender to rare-breed cattle. But they also have this beautiful resort, built around the old walled garden and the oast houses. I was staying in one of their cottages down there; they're charming.'

She passed the phone to Stacey, who scrolled while the others leaned in for a look.

'It looks stunning!' gasped Stacey. 'How have we never been here?'

'They're struggling with their profile,' admitted Evelyn. 'They just need a far bigger marketing budget. I swear, it could be a gold-mine. There's so much potential across so many channels. I'm helping them organise a party and dinner for press and influencers next week. Seb's hosting it —lord knows, he owes me a favour—and I have Siobhan Quinn styling the whole walled garden. I'm super excited. It's going to be magical, and the list of attendees is looking shit-hot—largely thanks to Seb, I have to admit.'

Elaine reached over and pulled the bottle of wine out of the cooler. 'It looks enchanting, darling. Do you have sponsorship for the party?'

Evelyn's head shot up. 'No. We don't. Are you interested?'

'Well, wouldn't you say it would be a fun fit for Château des Anges?' Elaine poured Evelyn a glass. 'Try it. I'm absolutely shameless. I've even ordered it here.'

Evelyn took a good mouthful of the perfectly chilled liquid. Château des Anges was one of the newer jewels in Elaine's crown, a beautiful biodynamic vineyard and olive farm close to St Tropez. The wine itself was delicious: light, crisp and delicately fragrant.

'Elaine, this stuff is divine. It's going down like water. Are you serious about sponsorship? The fit with Sorrel Farm would be fantastic.'

'I am. We're putting some decent marketing budget behind Des Anges for the summer season. It sounds like your friends' approach to farming matches that of the vineyard. I'd need to see the brief for the event, and the guest list, but if Seb's hosting it then I'm sold already. Shall we chat after lunch?'

Evelyn was thrilled. She was well aware that the costs of the party were putting a considerable strain on Jess and Zoe's already stretched budget—Siobhan Quinn's services didn't come cheap. Having Château des Anges sponsor the evening would ease the burden significantly. She couldn't wait to tell them.

OVER OYSTERS, Evelyn laid out her concerns involving Ed Chang.

'I've been doing this too long to worry that it's personal, but this guy is a shark. He's a numbers guy; people make him nervous because he can't run them through a risk model and pop out a figure.'

'What did he say to Seb?' Stacey asked.

'He was hacked off that Seb came out and put the brand in jeopardy, but we're through the other side now and he has to admit that the ensuing boost to our revenues has been massive. So now he sees me as the loose cannon—the pissed-off wife who's been cast aside and has lost her motivation to play nicely. He thinks I'm disengaged, and he's worried that if the divorce proceedings turn nasty, then I'm liable to sabotage the company in a fit of pique.

'Finally, I suspect I've lost my currency in his eyes. As a husband and wife team, we were good media fodder. Now Seb and Gino are the media's darlings! So really, he sees no upside to having me on board, and an unquantifiable amount of downside.'

'Then lets take all of those bullshit assumptions one by one and destroy them.' Nira ripped a bread roll savagely in half as she spoke, and the others howled with laughter.

'Jeez, can you take Nira along to the meeting as your pet pitbull?' asked Stacey.

'First, talk to me about the divorce,' ordered Nira. 'Where are you?'

'We're going to try mediation before we go down the lawyer route,' admitted Evelyn.

There was a collective intake of breath.

'Are you sure?' asked Elaine, looking concerned. 'There are sizeable assets at stake here.'

'We're sure. Things are amicable, amazingly enough, and Seb's not going to be a dick about this, seeing as he ruined my life,' said Evelyn. 'It worked for Gwyneth and Chris, so it's worth a try before we let the divorce lawyers take a huge chunk of the pie.'

'Ok,' said Stacey, 'but you guys need to do a convincing job of persuading Ed that you're further along on that path than you may actually be. As you said, it's all about eliminating sources of downside risk for him. And make sure your body language with Seb shows that you guys are still a powerful team.'

'Good advice,' said Evelyn. 'Next?'

'Motivation.' Nira jabbed a finger in her direction. 'You need to go in there hungry and upbeat. Ed may be there to bitch about your relationship, but you can control the conversation. Keep turning it back to how big the opportunity is and show him you're the one he needs to execute on all of it. Don't let him forget how strong your track record is here.

'Next. He sounds like a greedy bastard. Sit down with your finance team and see where there's upside potential in your forecasts. If you can walk in there with a financial model that looks twenty, twenty-five percent better for the next twelve months than the one he's been looking at, he's going to start seeing dollar signs, and you've successfully changed the narrative.

'And finally. How fucking dare he assume you've been put out to pasture and you're not relevant to the brand? Get some friendly journalists on board. Get yourself some great profile pieces and show him how relevant you still are. Fuckwit.'

Nira sat back and drained her glass.

Stacey slammed her palm on the table. 'And *that*, ladies, is how it's done.'

Elaine laid a hand on Evelyn's and said quietly, 'While you're breaking your neck to impress this guy, just don't forget to ask yourself, is this what you really want?'

24

Evelyn had packed up most of her and Eddie's belongings and left their bags by the front door. The heatwave had finally broken. Outside, rain was hammering down from a swollen sky, which made for a premature dusk. She wondered if the parched land could even absorb such a glut of water. Angus would be pleased. She'd hardly seen him at all since the previous week's working lunch. She'd been burning the candle at both ends, planning the party as well as putting the finishing touches to her own company's marketing strategy for the second half of the year. It had to be seriously compelling to persuade Ed Chang to keep her on.

Tonight she had dressed for comfort, layering her camisole and yoga pants with thick socks and a soft, pale pink sweater that fell off one shoulder. She and Eddie were watching *Mrs Doubtfire*. Evelyn had even lit the wood-burner, and it cast a rosy glow about the room. She'd grown fond of this little cottage; they both had. She'd enjoyed playing house, grabbing milk or butter from the dinky fridge and sitting outside with her morning coffee. It made her wonder why on earth they needed a nine-thousand-square-foot mansion with two basements and six bathrooms. It all seemed a little excessive for their needs, frankly. This cottage felt like a better fit for her new, downsized family of two.

One of the many things Evelyn loved about motherhood was experiencing the world through Eddie's eyes. It must have been over twenty years since she'd last seen *Mrs Doubtfire*, but watching Eddie howl with laughter and cover his face while gasping dramatically at some of the more excruciating moments was almost as entertaining as watching the movie itself. They sat curled up on the sofa together for most of the movie, the exception being during the sequence to Aerosmith's *Dude (Looks Like a Lady)*, when they indulged in some wild jumping and brandishing of air guitars.

The action had just moved to the restaurant scene, which was the climax of the movie, when there was a knock at the door.

'It's open,' Evelyn called, expecting housekeeping. The door opened, and there stood Angus in a dripping-wet mac and wellies.

'Oh my goodness!' She leapt off the sofa. 'Come in, come in! It's revolting out there!'

'Hi guys,' said Angus, gingerly stepping through the door. 'Do you mind if I…' He gestured to his wet things.

'Please, take them off! Here, let me help you. Eddie, pause the movie please, and say hello to Angus.'

'Hi Angus,' intoned Eddie dutifully, eyes still on the screen.

'Hey, buddy.' Angus shot him a smile while trying to remove his wellies without stepping off the doormat. 'Oh, *Mrs Doubtfire*! Wow, I haven't seen that movie for years. My sons loved it when they were your age, Eddie. Are you enjoying it?'

'It's awesome!' said Eddie. 'Me and Mummy were dancing when Mrs Doubtfire was hoovering the house!'

'Oh, really?' Angus raised his eyebrows at Evelyn. 'That I would like to have seen.'

She smirked at him. 'Tea?'

'No thank you; I'm fine. I just thought I would drop by and say... goodbye. See if you needed any help getting packed up.'

'We've been very organised, so we're all good thanks.' She studied him. He looked tired and subdued, but very handsome, in a navy cashmere sweater that she imagined would be exceedingly soft to touch. She thought of him trudging back to a dark, empty house in this weather. 'Will you watch the rest of the movie with us?' she asked. 'There's not too much longer to go.'

His face brightened. 'Why not? I could do with a laugh. Do you mind if I bring Charlie in? He's in the car.'

'Of course not,' said Evelyn. 'Eddie will be thrilled.'

With Charlie fetched and settled on the floor by Eddie's feet, they resumed the movie. The farce quickly ratcheted up as Robin Williams ran back and forth between the meals with his family and his boss. When he performed the Heimlich manoeuvre on Pierce Brosnan's character and his mask detached itself from his face, they all shrieked and buried their faces in their hands. Evelyn snuck a sideways glance at Angus while he laughed along. He caught her eye and grinned. She felt a rush of happiness to be sitting here, between these two.

When the credits rolled, Eddie hit pause. He was no longer laughing.

'Mummy, are you and Daddy going to get a divorce?'

Evelyn met Angus' eyes again. She turned back to Eddie and stroked his hair.

'We probably are, sweetie. Daddy will be happier with Gino than with me. I know it's a lot to take in. But we're still best friends, and we still run the company together. And look at what happened at the end of *Mrs Doubtfire*. Their mummy and daddy were much happier when they lived apart, and the kids got to spend lots of time with both of them. That's going to happen with us, too.'

She waited for some pushback, but Eddie just said, 'Can I take Charlie upstairs and show him my room?'

'Um, I guess so. Just don't tell Jess we had a puppy in the house! Ok?'

'Come on, Charlie!' He ran upstairs, Charlie eagerly in tow.

Evelyn groaned. 'Ugh. I should have seen that coming, after that particular movie choice.'

'You did great.' Angus paused. 'Come here.'

He put an arm around her and pulled her towards him. She leant her head on his chest. The sweater was as soft as she'd imagined. She pulled her feet up from the floor and swung her legs over his. With his free hand, he gently pushed her hair away from her face.

She burrowed in towards his neck and inhaled the scent of his skin.

'Angus?' Her voice was muffled.

'Mmm?'

'Do you think it's weird that we—hug—like this?'

He laughed. 'Evelyn. This is not hugging. I don't know what the fuck it is, but it's not hugging. I definitely don't hug anyone else like this.'

'But do you think it's weird?'

'Yes. It's extremely weird.'

'Do you want to stop?'

'Heavens, no.'

He ran his hand up her sweater sleeve, stopping at her bare shoulder and cupping it in his palm.

'I wish I'd met you in winter, when these exquisite shoulders of yours were safely wrapped up in lots of thick layers. It would have made life much easier for me. I've spent far too much time trying to ignore them, these past few weeks.'

She lifted her face slightly and kissed the side of his jaw. He had a couple of days' worth of stubble; it was surprisingly soft against her lips.

'Evelyn. Look at me.'

She raised her head heavily from its resting-place and looked at him. It felt miraculous, having permission to be so close to his face.

'Thank you.' He took her hand, his other arm still around her. 'These—moments—that we have together... they are some of the most intimate, enchanting, *extraordinary* experiences that I've ever had in my life. Ok?'

She nodded, eyes not leaving his face.

'I can't even tell you the kind of things I'd like to do to you right now. But I'm not going to do anything, and not just because your lovely little son is right upstairs. It's much more selfish than that—I'm afraid it comes down to good old self-preservation. You're going back to London in a few hours, to kick that fucking investor of yours in the balls, and you're going to kill it. You're going back to your life of running a successful company, appearing on the covers of magazines and taking private jets everywhere.'

She shoved him. 'We don't have a private jet.' Now might not be the best time to mention their NetJets Marquis Card.

'You know what I mean. You live a big, full-on life in a

world that I can't even imagine, and don't want to imagine, to be honest. I get up at four-thirty most mornings and spend my days literally knee-deep in shit.'

'Stop underselling yourself. You have a degree from Oxford, for God's sake. And what you're doing here is very inspiring, and so important.'

'Let's just say, I've been doing a little research on you.' He blushed, adorably. 'You are beyond impressive. It's fairly obvious that it's not your husband running the show, despite it being his name on the door.'

The image of him googling her up in his lonely home was unbearably poignant. Did he use reading glasses? She could imagine him pushing a pair of dorky specs up the bridge of his nose.

'The point is, I don't just want a night with you. Well, I do. Very much. But it would just make things a million times harder. You have an intense few months ahead of you. You're going to be enduring a divorce and adjusting to single parenthood while keeping your company moving forward. It's a big mandate. I know you'll do an amazing job, but your head needs to be in London, not here. And as soon as you get back there, you'll immerse yourself in it. I haven't made a move on you because it just makes everything way too complicated. I almost didn't come tonight, but it was too hard to stay away.'

She felt a bittersweet tangle of blissful relief that he'd acknowledged the intensity of the feelings that lay between them, and pain that their circumstances prevented them from acting on those feelings. 'I'm glad you came. Very glad, actually.' She hesitated. 'I wish things were different.'

He planted a soft, fleeting kiss on her lips and, gently disengaging himself from her, stood up. 'Me too, Evelyn, believe me.'

He and Charlie left a couple of minutes later. She watched him put on his sodden mac and boots and head out into the filthy night.

25

On the dot of six the next morning, Evelyn opened the front door of the cottage to load up the car. She'd already showered, meditated and taken her supplements. Might as well get back into that focused, professional mindset that had always served her so well. Eddie was still fast asleep, and her plan was to wake him at the last minute and put him in the car in his pyjamas. With any luck, he'd fall back to sleep.

She would leave the cases of wine and a few other bits in the cottage. She'd rented it straight through until the day after the party. It gave her a little more flexibility in case she had the inclination to flee back down here. It would all depend on how today went.

The rain had stopped at some point overnight, but it had left its mark. The temperature had dropped considerably, and the downpour had released the scents of the farm, so that the air smelt thickly of roses and white lilac.

She hadn't slept so well. It had been hard to find oblivion after Angus had left. Eddie had been quiet and clingy; the movie had likely got those little cogs whirring in his brain. In the end he'd slept in her bed, and she'd been glad of the warmth of his small body and the comforting regularity of his breathing.

She was loading the last of the bags when she heard a scampering noise. Charlie bounded over to her, jumping up on her in excitement.

'Charlie. Down. Hey there.'

Angus came into view. He was back in his standard shirt and gilet, despite the coolness of the morning. He had two cardboard coffee cups; he held out one.

'I took a chance that I might see you. And I took another chance on how you take your coffee. I know you think milk is *passé*, so it's just black.'

She giggled. 'How predictable I am. Wow, this is a treat.' She accepted the cup. 'I may just be able to function after this.'

'How are you feeling about today?'

'Ok, thanks. Determined. I'll spend the journey getting into the right headspace. Maybe I'll pop a Tony Robbins audiobook on in the car.'

Angus laughed. 'You'll walk in, punching the air. They won't know what's hit them.' He peered into the back of the car. 'Do you need help with Eddie?'

'I was going to wake him in a minute and bring him down.'

'I can carry him down if you want? Save waking him? I've had some practice recently.'

She shrugged. 'Well, that would be amazing. Thank you. He's—he's in my bed, actually.'

'I'll work it out, I'm sure.'

He returned holding a still-sleeping Eddie and his bunny and put him in the back seat. Evelyn watched as he expertly fastened Eddie's seat-belt around him.

'Muscle memory?'

He laughed. 'Something like that. I'm not sure it ever leaves you.'

He loitered until Evelyn had locked the door of the cottage and climbed into the car. She put the front window down.

'Thanks for seeing us off, and for this coffee—which is delicious, by the way. I didn't expect to see you this morning.'

His face was serious. 'I'm glad I took the chance.' He leant in through the window and kissed her on the cheek. 'Go and do what you need to do. I look forward to hearing all about it at the party.'

THE SKY WAS STREAKED with dark purple and pale gold, as the drama of the rainstorm yielded to the stillness of the new day. Evelyn punched her home address into Waze and settled in for the journey. Waze was showing a journey time of one hour thirty. No music. This was precious thinking time.

She should be working through how the meeting with Ed Chang would go, but her head was filled with Angus. How on earth had her feelings for him escalated so quickly? It was as if her subconscious had latched onto him right at the start, and her conscious mind had needed a little longer to catch up. All it had taken had been some incendiary comments from Jess, and a few almost mystical moments in his arms, and whoosh. Her heart had gone up like a tinderbox.

On the surface, they'd had very little interaction—they'd spent hardly any time together, and they hadn't even kissed properly. The entire situation was, as Jess had observed, very Victorian.

And yet, and yet. The strength of their connection didn't seem to depend on constructs of time and space. She felt as though she'd always known him, on some level. It was as though he could read her mind. She loved him. It was crazy, but true. And then at the less lofty end of the scale was her physical attraction to him. She couldn't believe how badly she wanted to be with him—it took her breath away. Last night, curled up in his arms on the sofa, she'd cursed their self-restraint and common sense. Fuck that. She wanted him to carry her off to bed. She remembered his voice, his words: *I can't even tell you the kind of things I'd like to do to you right now*. The look in on his face when he said it was burnt into her mind's eye. How on earth was she supposed to walk away from him?

Jesus. Get a grip. She would crash, at this rate. Think about something unsexy. Like how the hell she was going to save her job. If she pulled this off, she'd be so busy executing on this marketing plan that she'd have no head-space for mooning over lost loves. Her girls' lunch had really galvanised her. She'd gone soft during her few weeks in Kent. It had been wonderful, despite the circumstances, to have some time to laze by the pool, drink too much wine, eat carbs and soak up the beautiful surroundings. But lunch at the Arts Club had rekindled that professional fire in her.

Seb's bombshell had thrown her much further off course than she'd realised. Seeing the girls had reminded her who she was. She was driven and relentless and focused on excellence. That fire had carried her through so many dark times and had heightened the triumph of the good times. Ambition was her drug of choice.

She thought about the company she and Seb had grown

together, the all-nighters they'd pulled, the late-night calls with the US when Eddie was a newborn who didn't believe in sleep, the horrifying regularity with which things went wrong during their live events around the world. She thought about the Krug they'd popped open when they got their first round of investment, that Prince's Trust dinner when Seb cooked for the Prince of Wales, and Food magazine calling them the Beckhams of the food industry. They were seriously good together, because their ambitions were limitless.

After the last few weeks, she felt as though she was two different people. She craved the glitter of London society and the adrenalin rush of building and running a sizeable company. She wanted power-lunches with ballsy, dynamic girlfriends who all understood that ambition and insecurity were two sides of the same coin, two animals that needed to be kept on a tight leash. She wanted to fuel her brain and body with the cleanest foods to provide the physical and cognitive stamina that she needed to stay on top of her game. She wanted to excel, not for the rewards as much as for the sense of achievement. She wanted impact.

And yet, a part of her recognised this approach as unhealthy. By threatening to topple the life that she had built for herself, Seb had given her the gift of perspective, of an alternative way of living. She'd spent hours lazing around with Eddie, reading to him and watching him grow relaxed and golden—he'd thrived in his new surroundings. She'd eaten and drunk for the sheer, visceral pleasure it gave her, and to celebrate the bounty of nature as it cycled through the seasons. She had cast her judgement of food out the window, and just lived.

Granted, she'd gained a few pounds and a good deal of bloat, but it had been worth it. She'd laughed with friends, fallen head over heels in love, and listened to her intuition. For what was it but intuition that had told her to throw all of her social niceties out of the window and reach out to Angus that day in the lavender field?

She'd felt at one with nature, not apart from it. Being in nature, being close to the land and to the food that she was eating, suited her. It made her feel as though she was tapping into the source power of mother nature herself. On paper, the amount of gluten and alcohol she'd consumed at Sorrel Farm should have made her feel sluggish, but in fact she'd had a more abundant outpouring of creative ideas in the last fortnight than she'd had all year. When she'd thought about the opportunities that the farm presented for Jess and Zoe, she'd felt that familiar rush of adrenalin as the ideas tumbled out of her.

If only she could find a way to recognise and nurture both sides of herself within a single way of living. She wanted to safeguard the lessons she'd learnt about slowing down, listening to herself, and making space to enjoy life, while retaining the drive, the spark, that made her who she was.

She glanced in the rearview mirror and the solution came to her in a flash as bright as the rising sun behind her. It was a complete download, a perfect moment of understanding. Afterwards, she wouldn't quite be able to recall how everything had come together for her. It felt somehow right to be having this revelation on the M25, suspended in limbo between her two worlds, her two lives. And now, two phone calls were all that it would take to set the wheels in motion. She hit Seb's number on the dashboard console.

26

The first thing that struck her was the sheer size of her home. It felt like a beautiful museum, tastefully curated with elegant objects. Part of her thrilled at being back in this rarefied world where everything radiated a veneer of wealth; part of her wanted to turn and run.

Eddie had woken up as she'd turned off the ignition, and he emitted an ear-splitting shriek when his father came down the stairs. Seb was already dressed in a bespoke navy suit of lustrous Italian wool; it showed off his tall, slim frame to perfection.

'Daddy!' yelled Eddie, throwing himself into his father's arms and wrapping his legs and arms around him.

'If it isn't my little koala,' said Seb, planting smackers on Eddie's cheeks. 'Well, don't you two look well—all golden and rosy.' He kissed Evelyn on the cheek. 'Did you have a good run up?'

'Plain-sailing,' replied Evelyn. 'I'm going to go and put my armour on. I'll see you boys in the kitchen.'

EVELYN and Seb strode into Iguana Capital's Berkeley Street offices at 8.55am. Evelyn was glad they were arriving together; it was a powerful show of unity for Chang's benefit.

'Sebastian and Evelyn Macleod, to see Edward Chang,' Seb told the receptionist. She waved them through to the lift bank.

Once in the lift, Seb turned to her. 'Are you sure you want to do this darling?' he asked her, studying her face.

'I am. I wish I'd had this moment of clarity sooner, but my gut is telling me this is the right thing for me to do.'

'Then I'm with you all the way,' said Seb. 'It's the least I can do for you. I hope this will be a wonderful new chapter for you, Ev. Now, let's go and put Chang back in his box.'

THERE WERE eight people around the table: Ed Chang and his colleague, who'd come to take notes, the Macleods, their Finance Director, Rory, Elaine Williams, and two other non-executive directors, or NEDs—Michael Fishburn and Ali Nazari.

Evelyn was feeling confident. This was her natural habitat; these were her kind of people. The boardroom was on the fourth floor of Iguana's Berkeley Street townhouse. The sunlight streamed through the windows and hit the highly polished board table. Everything about the offices screamed wealth, from the glossy receptionists to the thick wool carpets and the serious art on the walls. It may all have been designed to intimidate, but it acted as an aphrodisiac for Evelyn. There was something about being in the thick of it in London, where the deals were done and the players made their moves, that galvanised her.

She knew she looked the part. To further reinforce the impression that she and Seb were a united, potent force, she'd matched him in a navy Emilia Wickstead jumpsuit and vertiginous heels. She'd pulled her hair back into a sleek chignon, and her gold armour was on. It was showtime.

Ed kicked off. 'The first order of business today is to discuss whether it's appropriate for Evelyn to retain an executive role within the company. Your abilities are not in dispute, Evelyn. But the shit-show that's been played out in the media has left the investment team at Iguana wondering whether you can hack the strain of it. You ran for the hills when the news broke and I have to say, we're questioning your commitment. We need someone who's a hundred percent focused on the opportunity here.'

Seb cut in. 'The shit-show, as you call it, was all my doing. So don't take it out on Ev.'

'Your name's on the door, Seb. You're not going anywhere. But we're highly sceptical that you guys can transition from a husband-and-wife leadership team to whatever your new relationship will be. I assume you're getting a divorce?'

'We are.' Evelyn's voice was calm. 'It's amicable, and it's progressing well.'

'Look,' said Ed.

Evelyn hated it when people started a sentence with 'look'. It was so patronising.

'Look. The brand we bought into has blown up. You guys spent a lot of time painting yourselves as the power-couple of this industry. That's gone. Now Seb's got a new guy, and Gino is supposed to work under you, Evelyn, and I'm supposed to believe that you're all going to play nicely at work? No fucking way. Something's going to blow, and it's going to put our investment at stake. Meanwhile, the brand is now in a vacuum where the Macleods as a couple are dust. So what are you going to do about it?'

He threw his hands in the air and looked at them accusingly.

'In that case, Ed,' interjected Ali, 'why don't you let Evelyn do her job right now and tell us what her marketing strategy is for the next phase?'

'Knock yourself out, Evelyn,' said Ed churlishly. Evelyn shot Ali a grateful look. She got to her feet and hit the return key on her MacBook, which was linked up to the big screen at one end of the room.

'The marketing strategy is simple. It's about honesty, integrity and wellness. One of the biggest insights we've had since Seb came out is that people have really responded to his willingness to address his flaws. He's showed that he puts an honest dialogue with his followers ahead of his self-image, and that's really resonated. So the book, *Honest Food*, has come to mean more than just real, whole, unprocessed food and the benefits it has for our bodies. It's come to stand for stripping back dishonesty and pretence in order to live a truer life.'

She hit return and brought up a graph. '*Honest Food* sales before and after our *Post* interview. You can see the boost; sales are normalising, but they're still healthier than before. Seb and I believe that the key to harnessing the opportunity here is a careful combination of what Seb does best—the clean, vital, authentic way that he cooks, and of what Seb has to offer as a person—the vulnerability that he's shown in opening up about his true self. To that end, I give you this.'

She hit return. The next slide was a mock-up of a book cover. It was a beautiful black-and-white photo of Seb, gazing into the camera. Above the image was one word —*Honest.*

'*Honest* is the obvious next step. It's part memoir, part manifesto for how to live, and part recipe book. Mind, body, soul, being true to yourself—this encompasses it all. It's a lifestyle bible, really. My recommendation is that we move quickly on this—Seb works with an experienced, and fast, ghost-writer, as our in-house team builds out the food and recipes section. The tagline could be something like '*Honest: my philosophy for life.*''

There was a murmur around the table.

'This is marketing genius,' said Elaine. 'They'll lap it up.'

'There's additional revenue stream I'd like us to consider,' Evelyn continued. 'Hotels. Seb's Kitchen does brilliantly. As we continue to up the ante on the wellness front, like expanding our supplement collaborations, having outposts of Seb's Kitchen in hotels, starting in London, would be a brilliant fit. We'd advocate targeting hotels with a high percentage of business travellers. Instead of spending forty minutes on a large hotel breakfast in the morning, these people can pop into Seb's Kitchen by the lobby and quickly fuel up for their day or their flight. The menus will reflect their needs. If you're fresh off a red-eye, we've got just the juice, supplement and breakfast combination for you. And we take it stateside within twelve months.'

'I like it. Show me the numbers,' barked Ed.

Evelyn hit return and Nick stood up. 'Here are our revenue forecasts, month-by-month out to the end of next year. The grey line shows our old projections. The blue line is adjusted to show the impact that the news cycle has had on sales so far. The red line extrapolates that and assumes we continue the PR offensive till at least the end of this year.

'Then, the green line assumes that the new book launches early next year, and that we get three Seb's Kitchen outposts open in the first half next year. Here's the full P&L forecast.'

Nick handed some printouts around the table.

'We need to schedule a follow-up to number-crunch on this,' said Ed, running a finger down the financial model. 'Nick, I need to understand the capital requirements that a hotel roll-out would involve. But Evelyn, this is fucking good. These are both big. They put us back on the front foot. Nice work.'

Evelyn was still standing. 'There's one more thing,' she said. Her heart was hammering against her ribcage.

'Oh yeah?' Ed's eyes were still on the page in front of him. He was furiously circling figures with his pen.

'I won't be here to execute any of this for you. I'd like to resign my position from the company and from the board.'

Ed looked up. 'What the fuck? That's not necessary, Evelyn. Have you been listening in this meeting? I'm going to give you a shot. We need you to execute this.'

'No, you don't.' Evelyn could feel Seb's silent support from where he was sitting. She went on. 'I want a clean break, a new challenge. This strategic plan is my parting gift. I have someone in mind to replace me—she's amazing. But you don't need me. And to that end, I'm going to sell down my entire stake in the company. I want to do this quickly, so I won't be seeking a new valuation. I'm willing to exit at the same valuation as the last round, even though you can see from these numbers that our top line is far outpacing the assumptions we used last time.

'I'm giving Iguana first refusal. You have forty-eight

hours to let me know if you want to take up the shares. If not, Seb will partially buy me out and I'll find another buyer for the rest. This is a good deal, Ed.'

She sat down and exhaled. She caught Elaine's eye and smiled with relief as the older woman silently punched the air.

27

The day of the Sorrel Farm party dawned, and Evelyn couldn't get down to Kent quickly enough. The week had passed in a flurry of conference calls and spreadsheets until she couldn't crunch another number. She took Eddie down to the farm as soon as rush hour had passed. Seb and Gino were due to meet them down there in time for the party at six.

She was surprised at how happy she was to walk through the door of her sweet cottage again. She'd spent most of the week in London working at her kitchen island, preferring it to the gentlemen's-club-vibe of their study. But this little place evoked pure leisure and happiness. She cast a wistful glance at the sofa. Last time she'd sat on it, she'd been entwined with Angus.

She dropped Eddie at Jess' house with Mike, Mia and the *au pair*. They would play some tennis and then spend the rest of the day scampering around and most likely hindering the party prep. Freed up, she wandered down to the walled garden, where the set-up had been underway for a couple of hours. She was in denim hot-pants, a white singlet and flip-flops, and was ready to get her hands dirty.

The garden was a jumble of caterers' crates full of china, buckets of flowers, and stacks of delicate white wooden chairs, all awaiting their proper place. The long dinner table, which was in reality three tables arranged end-to-end, was already dressed in its pretty cotton cloths, printed with a faint pattern of green leaves. It would be the perfect canvas for the flowers, herbs and glassware that Siobhan's team would put in place later.

Against one wall of the garden stood a huge oak trestle. Zoe had suggested that, rather than plate up the food in the kitchen, she and her team should arrange it on enormous platters outside. The waiting staff would then serve the food up from this makeshift counter and bring it over to the guests. The purpose of this format was to showcase the farm's fresh produce. Someone was styling the trestle right now, putting in place tree-trunk rounds of varying heights which would act as stands for the platters. Siobhan would add in plenty of greenery between them, and Evelyn didn't doubt that this vignette would provide a good deal of Instagram fodder for the influencers.

She saw Angus only once during the afternoon. He rushed into the garden and started when he spotted her. He kissed her politely on both cheeks.

'How did the meeting go?' he asked. 'Did you get what you wanted?'

Evelyn looked him in the eye. 'It went brilliantly, thank you. I got exactly what I wanted.'

His face closed off. 'Well done. I knew you'd do it. I'll see you later—I'm looking for Jess.'

She shrugged off the pang she felt at misleading him.

He'd know the full story soon enough. It was time for her to check in with Siobhan.

By five-thirty, Evelyn was fully transformed. Her hair stylist and makeup artist had come down from London to work their magic and, as always, she was in awe of their talents. She'd considered that professional hair and makeup might be considered a little high-maintenance for round here, but it was fairly standard when she was representing her brand at an event in London, and this was a momentous night for her. Besides, she had a good decade on most of the glossy young influencers who were attending, so she needed all the help she could get.

She'd known, almost since she'd conceived of the party, what she wanted to wear tonight. It was one of the simplest, but most jaw-dropping, dresses she'd ever seen, and it was yet to have its first outing. It was a full-length but very bohemian scarlet silk habotai gown by a sustainable British brand named Kalita. Its effectiveness lay in the fact that it worked as well on the beach as in a nightclub. It was extremely voluminous, with a deep flounce at the bottom, and when it caught the wind it billowed like a ship's sail. Its real impact, though, was at the back. The fine shoe-string straps gave way to an ultra-low scooped rear, which made it completely backless. The risqué effect was balanced out by the magnificently expansive skirt.

Evelyn had added just gold sandals and her gold hoop earrings. The dress itself did most of the work. Her hair stylist had coaxed her long, dark hair into soft, beachy waves, and her makeup was sensational—smokey eyes and an artfully smudged, semi-translucent scarlet lip. They'd given her the confidence boost she needed. She was unusually nervous, but then again, the evening that lay ahead had unusually high stakes on several fronts. She was sure she would have botched her makeup, had she been left to her own devices.

When the knock came at the cottage door, she was ready. There stood Seb, looking like a film star in a trademark sky-blue shirt that showed off his eyes.

'Fuck me,' he said. 'You look absolutely ravishing, Ev. I don't think I'm gay after all.'

She swatted him playfully. 'Tough. You had your chance. You blew it, remember? Where's Gino?'

'Still preening. He'll see us down there. Meanwhile, it's my honour to escort you to dinner. This is *your* night, my darling. Are you ready to go and do this?'

IT FELT strange to be walking into a party on Seb's arm, after everything that had happened. The last six weeks had felt like a lifetime. As they entered the walled garden, she gasped. It looked breathtaking; Siobhan had done a magical job. There were tubs and troughs of blue, purple and white flowers everywhere. Most magnificent of all were the towering delphiniums, in all their shades of indigo, periwinkle and lilac. A jazz band was playing softly in the corner, and groups of guests dotted the area around the pool. Evelyn accepted a glass of champagne from a waiter and drank in the scene. It was exactly as she had imagined it, and she knew that everyone who attended tonight would feel as enchanted as she did when they first walked through that old wrought-iron gate.

Jess, Zoe and Angus stood in front of them, chatting with

some early arrivals. She started to lead Seb towards them, but they were stopped by a few photographers who indicated that they wanted a photo. Siobhan had hired an official photographer for the evening, but Evelyn guessed that several of the broadsheet journalists had brought their own. They posed side by side, Seb's arm flung around her shoulders. They both knew that this would make the papers tomorrow—Seb Macleod and his soon-to-be-ex-wife, looking happy and relaxed together.

Photo op completed, they headed for Jess, who was waving them over. Evelyn's heart was thumping. It would be seriously weird introducing Seb and Angus, but at least Seb would be oblivious.

'Seb!' cried Jess. 'I fucking hate you, but thank you so much for coming. We're thrilled to have you.' She threw her arms around him.

'I fucking hate you too, Jess darling,' retorted Seb, kissing her, 'but you look stunning. And Zoe—Jesus, you get more beautiful every time I see you. I'm delighted to be playing second fiddle to you and your chefs tonight—it's just as it should be.'

'*Bienvenue*, dear Seb,' said Zoe in her husky voice. 'We're so happy to have you. Excuse me—I must run into the kitchen for a moment.'

Evelyn caught Angus' eye awkwardly. 'Um, Seb, this is Angus Rutherford. Angus is the farm manager here.'

'Great to meet you, mate.' Seb pumped Angus' hand vigorously. 'I'm very excited that we're getting our hands on your beautiful produce. I'd love to have a chat about it later, and I'm going to have a good look around the farm tomorrow.'

'How do you do, Seb,' said Angus, his voice measured. 'We're all looking forward to working with you.' He kissed

Evelyn on both cheeks again. 'Evelyn. You look wonderful.'

'She's a knockout, isn't she?' said Seb, looking at her admiringly.

'Seb! Evelyn! Darlings!' It was Hilary Fitzsimmons from the *Times*. She came towards them, arms outstretched.

'Oh, God help us,' Seb muttered. He put his arm around Evelyn. 'Excuse us, Jess, Angus. I think the schmoozing part of the proceedings has begun. Come on, Ev. It's time to work this place.'

28

It wasn't so much the tinkle of the fork against the wineglass that quieted the table, but the fact that Seb was now standing. As always, he had instant command of the gathering.

The dinner had gone off beautifully. Zoe and her team had surpassed themselves, producing platter after platter of deliciously fresh, simple food. There were pink lamb cutlets and crispy chicken legs, rosemary-roasted new potatoes and just-shelled peas with mint, crisp cucumber salads and verdant tabbouleh. Everything had come from the farm. The Château des Anges flowed throughout the meal. Elaine had been as good as her word, and her vineyard was the proud sponsor of the evening. Siobhan had allocated the pale pink bottles their own special bar, and they stood tiered with vases full of lavender and olive branches. The Château des Anges even made an appearance in the dessert, a light rosé jelly festooned with summer berries.

Evelyn had worked with Siobhan on the seating plan, careful to scatter the hosts evenly among the guests. She knew that they would all, in their own ways, bewitch their neighbours. They were the most persuasive advocates for the farm and its resort. She'd put Seb next to the Houston-based influencer, Arianna Rodriguez. She'd seen the woman in ecstasy over the garden earlier, snapping away at every rambling rose and table detail on her phone.

Meanwhile, British blogger Marjorie Lonsdale was sitting next to Gino. Gino was earning his keep, sending a steady stream of beautifully edited images to the official Seb Macleod Instagram Stories feed. Marjorie and Gino were giggling as they compared phone footage. When Evelyn checked her phone during a loo break, she saw that Marjorie was consistently re-posting Gino's Stories. That was excellent.

Evelyn had positioned herself between the *Tribune's* Sadie Thomas and a very sweet journalist from *Country Life* called Gerald. She could see Angus, towards the other end of the table, deep in conversation with *Food*'s Penny Hitchins. Penny was quite an earnest character, but was absolutely passionate about regenerative farming. Evelyn was fairly confident that she would fall under Angus' spell and feel compelled to evangelise at length on his farming philosophy in the pages of her magazine. That was the plan, anyhow.

The table itself was beautiful. She hadn't been quite sure how intimate the dinner would feel, given that it was still daylight, but the sun had settled into a soft haze, and the pool shimmered gently beside them. They'd lit candles anyhow—slim tapers that flickered, safe from the breeze, within tall, thin glass holders. The candle-holders were enclosed with rings of greenery, and vase after vase of purple, white and blue flowers dotted the table, mixed with small clay pots of rosemary, thyme and mint. As Evelyn had forecast, it looked and smelt wonderful.

'Ladies and gentlemen,' Seb began.

Evelyn's stomach was doing flip-flops. She took a gulp of rosé to steady her nerves. Her evening would soon become more momentous.

'I hope you're as thrilled as I am to be spending a beautiful summer's evening in such glorious, bucolic surroundings. I can tell you that as soon as I turned in through the gates of Sorrel Farm this afternoon, I felt my heart rate start to drop. This place is positively medicinal, and I'd like to thank its wonderful owners, Jess and Zoe, for their generosity in hosting us all here tonight.'

He turned and gestured to them, and there was a smattering of applause. 'If you've been reading the tabloids, you'll know that I've learnt a thing or two about honesty recently.' He paused to accommodate the laughter. 'Well, there is nowhere more honest than Sorrel Farm. Zoe and Jess have built their entire resort, and their whole farming philosophy, around authenticity. Most of us have complicated lives. When I come down here, I'm reminded of how simple life can be, and how pleasurable.

'At Sorrel Farm, I find food, straight from the gardens and the fields, such as we've eaten tonight. I find animals that are cared for and thriving. I find that nature has the upper hand here, and the team are here simply to do its bidding. I find enchanting surroundings, and hospitality based on straightforward human kindness. It's a very special place. Ev and I have been coming here for years with our son Eddie, and we're delighted that we can share it with you all tonight. We're also excited to announce that as of next month, Sorrel Farm will be one of our preferred suppliers. That means that we'll be able to share its produce with our visitors to Seb's Kitchen as well as at our corporate events. I hope this is the start of a long partnership for us all.

'And finally, I'd like to thank our sponsor, Château des Anges, for spoiling us with their delicious, biodynamic rosé. It's going down far too easily at our end of the table; I blame Arianna. And now, I'm honoured to hand over to our hosts, Jess and Zoe Augustin-Holmes.'

Seb kissed both women and took his seat to rapturous applause around the table. Evelyn's heart swelled. Practically all the influencers had been filming his speech on their phones. That footage would go straight to Instagram Stories around the world (she hoped Sorrel Farm's wifi could handle the barrage). The secret kingdom that her gorgeous, talented friends had created in this sleepy corner of Kent was about to go stellar.

Jess and Zoe stood up together. It was Zoe who spoke first. She looked radiant. This was a momentous occasion for them, too. Evelyn had sent her hair and makeup team to pamper them a little, before they tended to her. Zoe was wearing an intricate white Zimmerman maxi dress that Evelyn had lent her. It showed off her flawless, coffee-coloured skin and killer figure to perfection. Her light makeup enhanced her natural beauty, and her hair was wound around her head. She looked majestic. Oh boy, Evelyn thought, you'd better come around to the idea of being the face of this place, Zoe. You're the perfect poster-child for Sorrel Farm.

Zoe addressed the guests. 'Thank you all for joining Jess and I at our home tonight. We are so pleased to meet you all. I hope that you will find some time to relax and enjoy our farm while you are here. I would like to thank our farm manager, Angus Rutherford, for making Sorrel Farm the easiest and most pleasurable place in the world to be a chef. My team and I work with beautiful, vital food, and it tastes like it does because of the way it is grown or reared, not because of how it is cooked.

'Angus and I are committed to returning this land to its very best health. The farm is now fully organic, but we are passionate about regenerative farming, and our transformation to biodynamism is underway. We'll be continuing this process in the years ahead, and we are so happy to speak to any of you who wish to learn more about our processes. Thank you so much.'

Zoe took a sip of her drink and handed the mic to her wife, to the sound of applause.

Jess looked around the table. This was it, Evelyn thought. She smoothed out her dress.

'Thank you all so much for making the journey to be here. And thank you to our friends, Seb and Evelyn Macleod, for making tonight happen. Our hope, while you are here, is that you eat well, drink well, dance well, and that you discover the sense of wellbeing that the beautiful Kent countryside can afford you. Kent has been known as the Garden of England for hundreds of years, and surrounding us are miles and miles of fertile fields, orchards, and vineyards. For me, it's the most beautiful county in England.

'I grew up on this farm. It's always been a restorative place for me. All the work we've done on building this resort has focused on paying that sense of restoration and wellbeing forward to our guests. We believe that Sorrel Farm is a special place, with wonderful potential.

'To that end, I have some very exciting news to share with you all. Evie, come and join me.'

Evelyn rose from her chair and joined Jess. Jess put her free arm around her.

'Evelyn is my oldest friend. She's known Sorrel Farm for

most of her life. She's also the most talented businesswoman I know. Zoe and I can't think of anyone whom we trust more to help us guide this wonderful farm through the next chapters in its story. That is why I'm bursting with pride tonight. Evelyn will not only be our first outside investor in Sorrel Farm, taking a thirty percent stake in the company, but, effective immediately, she is stepping down from her role at Seb Macleod Ltd and joining us as our new Commercial Director.

'This is a role we've created specially for Evelyn. She'll be in charge of business development for both the resort and the farm, and she'll also run marketing for the time being. Welcome to the family, Evie! This is where you belong.'

Evelyn hugged her friend, elation and relief breaking over her. It was done. The crazy machinations of the past week had come good, and she was exactly where she wanted to be. She could sense, from the electric mood at the table tonight, that her instincts about Sorrel Farm had been correct. The press, and the influencers, were smitten. They'd fallen under the spell cast by Jess and Zoe in their enchanted garden. Evelyn would get to do what she loved and what drove her: building a business from its foundations and watching it fly. But she'd get to do it from a base that was removed from the frenetic, and sometimes toxic, energy of London, a place where she and Eddie could heal and thrive.

She looked around the table. The guests' faces were a mixture of surprise and delight. They were clapping and whooping. Seb was standing up, applauding her. That was sweet. He was her greatest supporter. They were so much better as friends. But there was only one reaction she cared about. This had been a gamble. She was utterly invested in her new role, her new opportunity. But if Angus didn't want her, then the taste of success would turn to dust in her mouth. She'd be lost. She didn't want to embark on this new life if it didn't include him.

There he was. Everyone else at the table became a blur. She met his eyes; they looked wet. She had the impression that, in that moment, no one else existed for him either. He was smiling at her, and his smile told her everything that she needed to know.

29

The table was cleared, and the jazz band gave way to a DJ. As the light started to fade, the fairy lights strung between the walled garden's fruit trees came on and the slate pool was illuminated from within. Guests thronged at the bar next to the pool, and Evelyn was swept up in a wave of goodwill and congratulations.

As soon as she'd sat back down after Jess' speech, Sadie Thomas had turned to her.

'I just found my next feature,' she'd said. 'Not some article on a jilted wife, but a profile on a woman who's taken a setback, pivoted, and created the most exciting new career opportunity for herself. My hat goes off to you, Evelyn. Please let me write this. We should put it in the Sunday magazine and shoot you right here.'

'I would love that!' Evelyn had laughed. It had been reassuring to hear that this seasoned journalist was as caught up in the excitement of her news as she was. And this kind of coverage would be worth its weight in gold to the resort.

She was chatting to Seb and Gino by the gleaming pool, when she saw Angus approach over Seb's shoulder. He looked so handsome tonight, in a white linen shirt open at the neck.

'Gentlemen.' He nodded to them. 'Do you mind if I steal my new boss away?'

'Be my guest,' laughed Seb, and they moved off.

She beamed at Angus. It was impossible not to. Her euphoria was rising further just at the sight of him.

He took her hand and stroked it with his thumb. 'Come over here with me? I'd like to have you to myself for a bit, if I may.' He led her to a quiet spot towards the corner of the garden, by a cluster of fruit trees.

'Congratulations,' he said, smiling down at her. 'I have to admit, I didn't see that coming. When you told me earlier you'd got exactly what you wanted, I assumed that meant you'd secured your role in London, and any window we may have had was firmly shut.'

'I knew you would have thought that, and I'm sorry.' She gazed at him steadily. 'I only worked out exactly what I wanted in the car on the way up to the meeting last week—after I left you. This solution is perfect. I can sink my teeth into this role, and it will fulfil my ambitious side, but it gives me and Eddie a new, healthier pace of life too.'

'I can think of other benefits,' he said. 'I assume you'll be basing yourselves down here?'

She felt herself blush. 'Yes, we will. It's going to be full-on for the rest of the summer, logistically speaking—new house, new school for Eddie, getting through the divorce proceedings... I'm sorry you had to find out alongside everyone else. It's been a crazy week, negotiating my exit from one company while simultaneously negotiating an investment, and a new role, with another one. I've been buried in spreadsheets all week, and Jess and I haven't been off the phone much.'

'I thought she'd been quiet this week,' said Angus thoughtfully. 'But I get it. You've had a lot to work through.'

'I came really, really close to calling you. I wanted your input... but I knew I had to make the decision without knowing how you felt. This had to be about my career, and about finding the right place for Eddie and me to settle. I was worried you might think that by moving down here I was being a bit...'

'... stalky?' offered Angus.

She laughed. 'Yes. Exactly.'

'Fortunately, I feel supremely comfortable being stalked by you. Stalk away. I won't put up any resistance at all.'

He ran his hands up and down her arms and looked down at her dress.

'My lady in red. You take my breath away. I could barely control myself when you walked into the garden with your husband. You looked like a film star.' He gestured towards the DJ. 'Shall we dance? I could request a bit of Chris de Burgh?'

She shoved him. 'Do that, and you'll need to find a new dancing partner.'

'That's ok. I might proposition Seb. I think I have a bit of a crush on him, actually.'

'You and everyone else here. Unfortunately, his tastes run younger and more Mediterranean than you. You're stuck with me.'

'That works. Dance with me.' He pulled her into his arms. She leant her head against the coarse linen of his shirt.

He put his arms around her, and they started to sway together.

'This dress of yours has a fascinating construction. The skirt could easily accommodate a family of four seeking shelter, and yet there's absolutely nowhere on the top half for me to put my hands, except on your bare skin.'

She giggled. 'That's never stopped you before.'

'*Touché*. But I've never had the delight of your entire back before.' He ran a hand up and down her back, stroking the hollow of her spine with his fingertips. 'It already feels like home,' he whispered. He fondled one of her straps. 'And is it just these two little straps keeping this enormous contraption up? If I slipped them both off your shoulders, what would happen?'

'The whole 'contraption' would fall to the ground, in one fell swoop,' she told him, 'but that's not going to happen. Not right here, in any case.'

'Wow. I see.' He swallowed hard.

She reached behind her back and stroked his arms. They were as taut and toned as they had been in her fantasies. 'Mmm,' she whispered dreamily.

He laughed. 'What was that for?!'

'That was for Past Evelyn. Past Evelyn has been dreaming about feeling up those arms of yours for weeks—since I first met you and Charlie outside my cottage, in fact. I clocked them at once. They're very, very fine arms. They actually make me feel weak at the knees.'

He looked down into her face and smiled. 'You have no idea how good it feels to hear you say that. In that case, you'll have to return the favour sometime and put on that tiny little top you were doing your yoga in—you also had it on when you'd been on your run. Poor old Past Angus has been imagining peeling that top off you for weeks now.'

She gasped, and a bolt of desire shot through her. She had a pretty clear idea of his feelings for her by now, but to hear him articulate them so graphically was beyond attractive.

'I'm sure that can be arranged,' she murmured. 'I wasn't aware you were so pervy.'

'Oh, you have no idea,' he laughed. 'And, while we're on the subject of confessions, I have something else to admit. I was devastated for you and Eddie when I saw in the paper that Seb had come out. But, I have to say, I also felt a glimmer of hope. I found myself wondering if you'd come back and whether I was in with a vague chance.' He held her more tightly.

As they danced, she thought of the brief moments they'd had together—that initial, shockingly intense time in her cottage, when she'd first felt his hands on her skin and the jolt of something indefinable in her heart. Then had come the embrace in the field, when the earth and sky had seemed to move around them and she'd had the sensation that they were a part of something larger, something universal. Fondest of all, though, was the memory of being on the sofa with him and Eddie, watching a movie in her comfy clothes and then lying in his arms. It hadn't felt like a one-off; it had felt like family. And now, here she was, completely free to be in those same arms. She couldn't quite believe it.

Angus' hand moved inside the dip at the back of her dress, and she suddenly became aware of where they were. It wasn't yet dark enough for privacy.

'Angus. There are a lot of journalists and people with phones around here, all in search of a good story. I don't know about you, but I'd rather not give them that tonight.'

He looked up, appearing to notice their surroundings for the first time. 'Yup. Let's get you out of here—if you can sneak away from your own party?'

She laughed. 'Seb can hold the fort. Something tells me he and Gino will be in the pool before long, most likely in matching speedos. That should hold everyone's attention.' She paused and looked at him. 'We can go to my cottage.'

'Are you sure? What about Eddie?'

'Um, he's staying at Jess' tonight, actually, so Aurelie can babysit him and the others.'

'I see. So you're telling me you've got the cottage to yourself?'

'Yes.'

His hazel eyes flashed, and he bent his forehead to hers and groaned. 'Jesus Christ, Evelyn. Then what are we waiting for?'

THEY COULDN'T EVEN HOLD off till the cottage. As soon as they were beyond the walled garden's gate, Angus pulled her towards him, and kissed her deeply, his arms wrapped around her as if he intended never to let her go. Her head was swimming; her senses were full of him. She was fairly sure he was holding her up, and if he let her go, she'd collapse in a heap on the ground. If this was what his kisses could do to her, what on earth would it be like to be in bed with him? Seb had never, ever kissed her like this. It came to her in a flash that this was how it should be with a man, that she hadn't been properly desired in years. She had a feeling Angus was about to help her make up for lost time.

SHE STOOD with him in the bedroom of her little cottage. Angus took her face in his hands.

'Sweetheart. Before anything else happens, I need you to know that I am not messing around here. I don't do flings, especially not with my colleagues. I can't believe you're here to stay, that you'll be putting down roots here. If you were going back to London tomorrow, this would not be happening, and you should know I would be a broken man, just like I've been a broken man all week.' He kissed her. 'Thank you for coming back and saving me.'

EVELYN WAS as good as her word. When Angus' hands reverently slipped both straps off her shoulders, her dress did indeed slither effortlessly to the floor. She stepped out of it, and he proceeded, with admirable focus and quite spectacular skill, to demonstrate to her exactly how it should feel to be a woman in the hands of a man in love with her.

30

She awoke, lying on her side. He was pressed along the full length of her body, his chest against her back, his knees tucked in behind hers. His hand held her to him; his fingers splayed protectively on the soft skin of her stomach. His chest rose and fell steadily against her as he slept. It felt nothing short of miraculous to be here with him after the longing of the previous weeks.

The previous night, she had quite literally come back to life. She couldn't remember how long it had been since she'd denied herself the permission to recognise and act on her own desires, but during her decade with Seb she'd gradually subjugated her needs and buried them deep within her. Presumably, her subconscious had decided that it was less painful to do so than to question the shortcomings of her marriage. Now, she felt as though she was unleashed.

While her night with him had been a revelation, this seemed almost more precious—to be lying here, in his arms. To sleep with someone—the literal act of being asleep with someone—was to be at your most vulnerable. And here, beside her, lay this man who seemed to adore her, and whose kindness took her breath away. His forearms might make her weak, but she'd fallen in love with him because of his many quiet, small kindnesses. In that way, he was very different from Seb, who was the king of the grand gesture. Angus, she understood, would simply always be there for her—a constant presence when she needed him.

She recalled his carrying Eddie home from Jess' dinner, and then down to the car on the morning of her board meeting. She remembered his offer to distract Eddie on the farm after Seb's news had broken. He'd turned up when she'd most needed some quiet support, on the night before the meeting and again the next morning, with a simple cup of coffee. It seemed to her that his understated reliability was one of the most precious things about him.

She wanted to watch him sleep. She gently removed his arm from around her waist and turned over so she was facing him. God, he was so beautiful. She felt a rush of love, as well as the sacred gravity of her responsibility to care for him in the way he deserved. He was such a good man; he was entitled to the love of a good woman.

He stirred a little, and she reached up and stroked the side of his face, his neck, his shoulder. She already knew that she would never, ever tire of his skin. He opened his eyes, and a slow smile spread across his face at the sight of her. She sighed inwardly with relief. No matter what happened with a guy, there was always a tiny part of you that wondered, as The Shirelles had so famously articulated, if he would still love you tomorrow.

'Mmm.' He stretched and slid an arm around her. 'What a sight to wake up to. How did you sleep, sweetheart?'

She beamed at him. She couldn't help it. 'I slept like a baby, thanks to your handiwork last night. How are you feeling?'

He raised himself up on one elbow and looked down at her, his eyes roving over her face and body. 'I'll show you,' he murmured, 'exactly how I'm feeling.'

Some time later, Angus headed down in his boxers to avail of the cottage's Nespresso machine. He reemerged, set Evelyn's coffee down on her bedside table, and sat on the side of the bed, sipping his.

'It feels symbolic,' he said, 'to be able to bring you coffee in bed. I'm not sure I've ever felt so wretched as I did that night last week, leaving you on the sofa and heading off into the pissing rain. I was so fucking conflicted; I'd convinced myself I was doing the right thing by walking away from you, but nothing has ever felt less right.

'And the next morning, when I fetched those coffees from the Oast House and had to wave you off, I just couldn't stop thinking that that wasn't the way it should have been. I should have stayed that night and I should have been bringing you coffee in bed the next morning, not delivering it to your fucking car.' He laughed and dropped a kiss on her bare shoulder. 'Clearly, I've erased the presence of poor little Eddie from the entire story. I realise I couldn't have stayed, but I'm sure I could have squeezed in a lot more action on that sofa. The point is, I shouldn't have let you leave that morning without making a proper play for you. I'm sorry.'

Evelyn thought back. 'I felt just as shitty as you, but you were pretty honest about your feelings that evening. Don't be so hard on yourself. You thought I wanted to go back to my life in London, so you stood down. I think that's honourable, actually. I should be the one apologising for letting you stew for the past week. I just wasn't sure if I could pull everything off.'

He grinned sexily. 'Yup, it's going to take you a long time to atone for that. I must say, the party got off to a rough start for me, watching you and Seb doing your thing—I felt like a mortal who shouldn't get too close to the gods. And I usually hate surprises, but I have to hand it to you: last night was the best night of my life.'

'Big relief.' She smiled. 'It was the best night of my life too, no question. Now, I have a zillion WhatsApps from Jess, demanding salacious details. Do you want to put her out of her misery and head over there for breakfast? They're offering bacon and eggs.'

'Why not? Somehow, I seem to have worked up an appetite. I need to zip home and get a change of clothes—it's five minutes away. Shall I see you there, or...?'

'I'll wait for you here.' She looked at him steadily. 'Let's go over there together.'

THEY WANDERED over to Jess and Zoe's farmhouse, his arm slung over her shoulders. He'd reappeared at the cottage in a pale blue polo shirt over some navy swim shorts. Evelyn had showered and left her hair to dry naturally, pulling on a white, off-the-shoulder maxi dress. Angus clearly had some kind of shoulder fetish, and she certainly wasn't going to deny him his fix.

'I guess we should play it cool, if Eddie's there?' he enquired.

'Apparently Aurelie's taken the kids down to the pool for a swim and an ice cream—they had breakfast a couple of hours ago. So, there's no need to play anything cool.'

'Thank God. I've had enough of playing it cool to last me a lifetime.' He kissed her damp hair. 'The past few weeks of repressing my feelings have nearly finished me off.'

'Me too. Jess said our whole dynamic was very Victorian.'

'I don't disagree. But I think we put the Victorian phase of our relationship quite conclusively to bed last night; wouldn't you say?'

She giggled and wrapped her arm around his waist.

The front door of the farmhouse was open, and they walked through to the garden.

'Morning,' Evelyn called, somewhat self-consciously.

Jess shrieked and came running out of the kitchen. 'You two! Come here. Just—come here.' She put an arm around each of them and kissed them both. 'Tell me it's true. Please say it's true.'

Evelyn laughed and hugged her friend. 'It's true.'

'Yes!' Jess released them and clapped her hands together. 'About fucking time. I'm not sure Zoe and I could have stood another day of either of you moping around. Angus was like fucking Heathcliff this week,' she told Evelyn. 'And this one,'—she gestured at Evelyn—'has been a mess on all our phone calls. So thank Christ you finally got it on. Now, come and tell me everything.'

'Your discretion does you credit, as always,' Angus laughed. 'You won't get any dirt from me, though. I'm off to help Zoe in the kitchen. Good luck, sweetheart.' He squeezed Evelyn's hand and headed to the house.

Jess turned to Evelyn and hugged her once again. Her eyes were wet.

'Oh, my darling, darling girl. I can't tell you how thrilled we are for you. You're our two favourite people. Are you happy?' She gazed intently at Evelyn.

'I'm ecstatic,' admitted Evelyn, shrugging. 'I can't quite believe it. I feel like I'm on drugs, or something; I'm high as a kite.'

'Nobody deserves that more than you. Now tell me this, quickly, before they come out. Did those celestial choirs make an appearance last night?'

Evelyn blushed. 'Oh yeah. They sang the goddamn *Hallelujah Chorus*.'

ZOE LAID a platter of bacon and scrambled eggs on the table. Angus was behind her, carrying a tray of tea and toast.

'*Allez*,' she said. 'Please, dig in. *Bonjour*, Evie.' She kissed Evelyn on both cheeks. 'I'm so happy you guys had a fun time last night.' Her eyes danced. She was far more discreet than her wife.

They settled around the table, helping themselves to food. Angus poured out the tea and sat down next to Evelyn, putting a tanned arm along the back of her chair. It was a casual proprietary gesture, but it made her whole body thrill.

So.' Evelyn piled scrambled eggs onto her toast. 'Any feedback from the party? How do you think it went? I haven't—I'm afraid I haven't had much of a chance to catch up on social media this morning.'

Jess snorted. 'No surprise there, you shameless hussy. But don't worry about it. Our Instagram account has been buzzing with notifications all morning, which makes a refreshing change.'

'Gino sent me a WhatsApp to tell me your Instagram followers have tripled since yesterday! It's off quite a low base, but it's a brilliant sign. And you'll continue to see a build over the weekend. Any of the guests promise anything?' She took a bite of egg on toast.

'We caught up with Seb towards the end of the evening, and he mentioned that Arianna wants to do a full lifestyle post on the resort,' said Zoe. She's staying for the weekend, so I said she could spend some time in the kitchen with us.'

'And Penny said she's keen to get us into *Food*'s organic issue,' Angus offered.

Evelyn snorted. 'I bet she is. With you on the cover, staring broodingly off into the distance, no doubt. Great work, honey.'

Jess raised an amused eyebrow at the endearment. 'Yep, poor old Penny looked very forlorn after you two had scarpered. Speaking of which, Seb noticed you'd done a runner too—he was hoping to catch up with Angus, actually. I may have given him a few not-so-subtle clues about what was going on, but he seemed happy for you, to be fair to him.'

'Oh well,' said Evelyn airily. 'I found out about Gino from some paparazzi shots, for God's sake, so I'm sure he wasn't expecting me to ask for his blessing when I moved on.'

Much to Jess and Zoe's obvious delight, Angus leant over and kissed her deeply on the lips. 'Right then, my little adulteress. It seems I have a fun conversation with your husband to look forward to later. We can discuss how he feels about his company becoming our largest customer while I run off with his wife.'

'I never, ever thought I'd say this,' said Evelyn, 'but right now I'm feeling pretty bloody grateful to Seb, and to the *Post*, for the way everything's worked out. Here's to Seb.'

They raised their teacups. 'To Seb.'

Hindsight was a gift, indeed.

EPILOGUE

She stretched out luxuriously on the old wooden bench. Sunday morning, and she had nowhere to be but right here in this charming, bountiful garden. In the fruit trees above her, the birds competed with each other for the airwaves. Charlie sat by her feet, dozing in the morning sunshine.

She picked up her phone. There was a WhatsApp message from Seb with a photo of him, Gino and Eddie at some superhero-themed film premier in Leicester Square the previous evening. They were all wearing black tie and had their hair slicked back in identical styles. She zoomed in; Eddie looked both adorable and ecstatic. He had plenty of new father-figures in his life, as well as a new puppy, which suited Evelyn perfectly. At least Charlie was already house-trained.

Checking her email, she scrolled past the confirmation letter for Eddie's new school. In about six weeks he'd be starting at a lovely, nurturing prep school in Sevenoaks. It was co-educational and had plenty of green space—unlike in London, where twenty grand a year got you a square of astroturf behind a cramped townhouse.

She clicked on an email from Monica, her property consultant. Monica's mandate was to find a large period property, ideally Georgian, with at least a couple of acres, an outdoor pool and a tennis court. She'd sent through a couple of initial options, properties that weren't technically on the market but that might be sold for the right price. One in particular caught Evelyn's eye. It was a gorgeous, wisteria-clad manor house in Ightham, near the historic Ightham Mote. It was only a few miles away from both Sorrel Farm and Sevenoaks.

It ticked all of her boxes, but its prize asset was a small, walled kitchen garden. In her mind's eye, she saw Eddie growing tall and bonny in these grounds, bringing his friends home for tennis matches and pool parties. She saw the old barn-like structure, which had apparently been a cowshed at one point, transformed into a stunning pool-house. Most clearly of all, she saw herself and Angus, sitting out on the west-facing terrace with a glass of chilled white wine, watching the sun set (after he'd tended to the produce in their kitchen garden, of course. That would most definitely be his department).

The last two weeks had been a whirlwind. She and Eddie were technically still based at the Sorrel Farm cottage. It was a little ridiculous, spending the summer in what should be a weekender cottage, but its location, easy size and daily housekeeping service made it the perfect pied à terre. Jess and Zoe had been godsends, treating Eddie to numerous sleepovers so Angus and Evelyn could have their fill of each other at the cottage, or here, at Angus' peaceful home.

Both women had seemed to be walking on air over the

past fortnight. Jess was prone to welling up when she saw moments of affection between Evelyn and Angus, and sundowners as a foursome at the girls' farmhouse had become a regular habit. Evelyn had carried out a further raid on the Holland Park wine cellar. Zoe and Jess were also deservedly revelling in this period of optimism around Sorrel Farm, when the media buzz was showing no sign of abating and the resort was steadily getting booked up for summer. With several million pounds of investment imminently hitting their bank account, they could sleep easy for the first time in a while.

It wasn't all rock-and-roll, given Angus' four-thirty wake-up time most weekdays. But they talked and talked and talked. When she could get away with it during the workday, she followed him around the fields, catching up his forty-six years on this earth as well as quizzing him on his stretch-targets for the land, his machinery capacity and his budgetary requirements. She wanted to know every detail about him; they had so much lost time to make up for.

She'd already met his sons, Hector and Alistair, home from university for the summer and living with their mother in Sevenoaks. She'd also met Audrey, who thankfully looked nothing like her famous namesake. Angus' boys were exactly what she'd expected—good looking, charming, bright, and impeccably mannered. They were also wonderful with Eddie. There was a plan for the five of them—and Charlie—to head down to a fabulous rental she'd found in Devon for a week in August, so that they could bond fully. Then she and Angus would hand Eddie over to Seb and indulge in a few nights down in Cap d'Antibes. No work, no pre-dawn alarm—just the two of them.

She sat up straight as he came into the garden, carrying

a breakfast tray and the Sunday papers. He was in shorts and a t-shirt.

'Coffee, croissants and—ta-da! The *Tribune*!'

He laid the tray carefully at the end of the bench and sat down beside her, kissing her.

'You popped out for it? You're an angel.'

'Of course I did! Open it—I can't wait to see it.'

She pulled the plastic-wrapped package of supplements from the middle of the folded paper and tore it open. There it was—her feature. Sadie had done her proud. On the cover of the *Tribune's* very popular Sunday magazine was a photo of Evelyn, posing in the walled garden wearing an enormous, frothy, pale pink Giambattista Valli Couture gown and leaning on a rake. The garden had been styled with an abundance of extra pink and white flowers brought in for the shoot. The effect was out-of-this-world.

The title below the picture was one word: *PHOENIX*.

'Bloody hell.' Angus picked up the magazine for a closer inspection. 'That's incredible! You look like a goddess. And check out the garden! Our little farm looks world-class.'

'It is world-class.' She jabbed at the photo. 'And this is the article that will launch a thousand reservations, mark my words.'

Angus thumbed through the magazine to find the article and started to read. It turned out that she'd been wrong about his needing specs.

'Here we go. Let's see... *Earlier this year, you may have been forgiven for assuming that Evelyn Macleod's gilded life was over when her husband, celebrity chef Seb Macleod, came out as gay in a tabloid. You could not have been more wrong. In the two months since then, Evelyn has resigned from the brand she built up with her husband, selling her stake in the company to their principal investor, Iguana Capital. She has relocated to Kent, where she has invested in and taken up the role of Commercial Director for an old friend's charming hotel, resort and organic farm, Sorrel Farm.*

'The resort is already that rare combination of luxurious and earthy. At just over an hour from central London, it deserves to be on the map. Given Evelyn's flawless track record and magic touch at Seb Macleod Ltd, we can be confident that Sorrel Farm's rise will be similarly stratospheric in her capable hands.

'Wow! Sweetheart, this is amazing stuff! Jess and Zoe are going to be very happy women.' He dropped the magazine, and cupping her face in his hands, he kissed her.

'It looks like the rest of the article lays out your strategy for building out the resort, but there's also a lot of focus on our plans for the farm and our transition to biodynamism,' he continued, scanning the pages.

Our plans. She and Angus, and Jess and Zoe, would grow this wonderful farm together. They'd make it a roaring success and a household brand. And at the end of the day, when her brain was fried and his body aching, they'd come home and make each other whole.

'We're going to do it together, darling.' Her eyes shone brightly. 'This is our time. Now, for the love of God, please pass me one of those croissants.'

AFTERWORD

All of the characters in this book are fictional, with two exceptions:

Our naughty show cocker spaniel puppy, Charlie has, for the purposes of this story, morphed into a slightly more competent version of himself: a working cocker. The command we give most often to him is, indeed, 'down'.

Evelyn's son Eddie is based on my nine-year-old son, Paddy. I had both permission and input from Paddy for the character.

Meanwhile, my seven-year-old daughter, Tilly, has not been immortalised in the book and is absolutely furious about it. I've had to promise to put her in the next one. You have been warned.

A NOTE FROM SARA

Thank you so much for taking the time to read this book.

If you enjoyed it then I'd be extremely grateful if you could take a moment to review it on Amazon.co.uk.
As I've published *Food for Thought* independently, recommendations and reviews are its life-blood.

Thank you, and I hope our paths cross again soon!

Sara

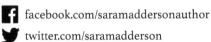

 facebook.com/saramaddersonauthor

 twitter.com/saramadderson

 instagram.com/saramaddersonauthor

ACKNOWLEDGMENTS

A huge thank you to the good folks who've helped me and held my hand through this double adventure of writing, and self-publishing, my first novel!

Thank you to my wonderful book cover designer, Caroline Taylor. Caroline created a cover that was perfectly 'me' and managed to see inside my head.

Thank you everyone who read drafts of *Food for Thought* and gave incredibly helpful feedback.

Particular thanks goes to my sisters, Louise Leandro and Jill Lee, who read every chapter as it landed and motivated me to write this book far more quickly than I otherwise would have!

I'd also like to thank my dear friend and beta-reader Wendy Harris for her wonderfully detailed and insightful notes.

ABOUT THE AUTHOR

Sara Madderson is an author, entrepreneur, wife and mother. She was born in Ireland and moved to the UK with her family when she was ten years old. She lives in London with her husband Chris, their two children, Paddy and Tilly, and their cocker spaniel Charlie.

Before turning to writing, Sara worked in finance for a decade and then ran her own fashion brand, Madderson London, for eight years. She earned her MPhil in Early Modern History from the University of Birmingham.

Food for Thought is Sara's first novel. She has previously published a non-fiction book focused on personal development, *Metamorphosis*.

Printed in Poland
by Amazon Fulfillment
Poland Sp. z o.o., Wrocław

61806891R00157